JAKE & THE NEFARIOUS GLUB

G.A. FRANKS

Copyright (C) 2020 G.A. Franks

Layout design and Copyright (C) 2020 by Next Chapter

Published 2021 by Next Chapter

Cover art by CoverMint

This book is a work of fiction. Names, characters, places, and incidents are the product of the author's imagination or are used fictitiously. Any resemblance to actual events, locales, or persons, living or dead, is purely coincidental.

All rights reserved. No part of this book may be reproduced or transmitted in any form or by any means, electronic or mechanical, including photocopying, recording, or by any information storage and retrieval system, without the author's permission.

For Daisy & Skye

Warning!
DO NOT READ THIS BOOK...

...If you are boring, easily offended or upset by gross things! This book has all kinds of yucky grossness in it. Things like pukey sick, toilets, poo and giant smelly farts! If I was you, I would close it right away and go and read a nice book about flowers and puppies and kittens instead.

Or...

You *could* take it to school and ask your teacher to read it out loud to the whole class! Tell them it's a heart-warming tale about a young boy who discovers the magic of reading, which is *technically* true — this book does have both magic and reading in it! Then you can watch their face when they get to the bits where they have to read out words like 'poo' and 'fart' and have to make unpleasant noises like PAAAARRRP! And you and your whole class can all have a good laugh at your boring old teacher being made to say rude things!

(But don't tell them it was my idea!)
G.A. Franks

Who's Who in Bisby by the Sea

Mrs Starling

JAKE

Lucy Starling

Sprat Starling

AJAY

Beryl Broom

Mrs Crisp

Prologue
(THAT'S THE FANCY NAME FOR THE BIT AT THE START OF THE BOOK BEFORE THE ACTUAL STORY GETS GOING!)

JAKE STARLING IS eleven years old and sees the world a little differently to most people. He sees it in Jake's way, and that's the way he likes it. He lives with his mum Daphne Starling, his big sister Lucy Starling and their pet dog Sprat Starling. (Sprat is a miniature schnauzer who enjoys doing doggy things like sniffing other dogs' bums and getting covered in mud and then running into the house and shaking it off all over the carpet!) The Starling family all live together in a big house in a place called Bisby by the Sea. Which, as the name suggests, is a town called Bisby and it's by the sea.

Bisby by the Sea is a very interesting and beautiful place to live. All the houses are painted in wild and wonderful colours and the harbour is always full of fishing boats with names like 'Evergreen' that bob up and down and bump into each other with a hollow *clonking* sound that keeps you awake at night, but in a nice way. Everywhere in Bisby smells of seaside and fish and chips, and the narrow, cobbled streets are like a maze, only with lots of hills and tunnels and hidden places to explore. Bisby by the Sea is even an interesting place to live in the winter, when the tourists have all gone home. That's when ice-cold waves smash into the rocky coast and mysterious fog rolls in from the sea, blanketing the whole of Bisby bay in a thick soupy mist. A small island called Clod sits just off the coast of Bisby, you can take a boat trip there if the sea is calm. Clod has many secrets of its own, and there is a ruined castle and some smugglers caves to explore. So, as you can see, Bisby by the Sea really is the perfect place to live. But — and this is a very big *but* — it is also a very, *very* strange place indeed. A strange place filled with some very interesting people, and where all sorts of unusual things happen!

1

The Best Teatime of the Year

IT WAS AROUND TEATIME when things started to go wrong for Jake. He had just finished his last day of school before the summer holidays, so it should have been the best teatime of the whole year. (Except for maybe Christmas Eve — but not Christmas Day. Christmas Day teatime isn't actually that good, because all the presents are already opened and Nana always wants to watch the Queen, but the Queen is really boring and teatime means that Christmas day is nearly over, which is rubbish because then its ages till Christmas again.)

But Jake had decided that this was definitely a great teatime because he had the whole of the summer holidays stretching out in front of him — six whole weeks with no school! That was one thousand and eight hours without having to listen to Miss Pillsbury bang on about boring school stuff! (He knew it was one thousand and eight hours, because he had checked.) Six weeks was *ages*, it might as well have been forever. Every playtime for the last month had been spent with his best friend Ajay, planning trips to the beach, or to the park by the lighthouse, or into the fairy woods in the chine at the top of the hill.

They had even planned a boat trip over to the Isle of Clod.

As was his way, Jake gleefully tore off his school tie and tucked into the worst bits of tea first, to get them out of the way quickly. The celery was swiftly dealt with, but he hadn't even got as far as the pork and pickle pie, let alone the crisps, when the best teatime of the year suddenly turned into a complete disaster.

'I've signed you up for a summer holiday reading competition at the town library,' breezed mum, in that special tone of voice that mums use sometimes that sounds cheerful but actually has a dangerous edge to it. 'All you have to do is read three books during the holidays and you win a bag full of fantastic goodies,' she beamed, enthusiastically waving a leaflet around. 'Look, if you take part you get stickers and bookmarks and even a video game...you love video games!'

Jake's heart sank. Deep down he knew she meant well, but — considering they are supposed to be so clever — it's no secret that sometimes grown-ups can be really stupid! 'Mum,' he whined, eyeing the leaflet suspiciously. 'It won't be a proper game; it'll just be some rubbish old computer program thing. It's probably called something really dumb like '*Super fun reading adventures*' or something!'

Before he had even finished speaking, Jake knew he was in trouble, but he couldn't stop himself. Sometimes he got what he called 'the urges.' They would build up inside him and he was powerless to stop them. Mum and Miss Pillsbury both said he should  try to ignore them and to think calming thoughts, but when he tried, the urge wouldn't go away. It would just build and build, making him feel all twitchy and irritated until he let it out. Sometimes the urge might be to do something, or touch something, or — like this time — say something. Before Jake could stop himself, the urge won, and angry words started to just sort of…fall out of his mouth. Even as he was speaking, he imagined a tiny version of himself standing on his tongue, desperately trying to catch the words in a net before they could escape. But the 'Mini-Jake' was too slow and all the words got out and Mum got cross and tea was ruined.

'Well I've signed you up now and you're doing it,' she snapped. 'You can't spend all summer not doing any reading, what

Mrs Starling

would Miss Pillsbury say?' Jake considered this for a moment. He wasn't actually sure what Miss Pillsbury would say. He knew she wanted him to read when he was at school, because she was his teacher and he was her pupil and it was her job to make sure he kept up with his reading. But for the life of him, he couldn't decide what she would say about him taking part in a library reading competition during the school holidays. If anything, he was fairly sure that Miss Pillsbury would probably just tell him to go away so that she could get on with enjoying her own holiday away from teaching him. (Jake knew full well that sometimes Miss Pillsbury found him a bit difficult at school, because he would ask the wrong questions…or too many questions…or no questions at all if he didn't feel like talking because the other pupils were being too noisy and one more voice would just make things worse.)

In the time it had taken him to consider this, mum had already started banging coleslaw onto her plate in a really noisy way so that everybody knew she was upset. Even though she knew that he hated loud noises, and that it was already obvious that she was upset, *and* that neither the plate nor the spoon of coleslaw was in anyway at fault. 'I do read,' said Jake after the banging had stopped. 'I'll read my graphic novels like I always do. There's a new 'Claws of the Dragon' book I want to read and…' Mum cut him off with one of her '*tutsighs*'. A tutsigh is a special 'mums only' sound that starts out as a disapproving 'tut' before turning into a long and melodramatic sigh. Jake was sure it was her favourite sound, because she did it so often.

'Jake!' she said in her 'firm' voice — he already knew what was coming. 'I've told you a thousand times,' (Which wasn't true, he hadn't been counting, but it was definitely NOT a *thousand* times, that would just be silly and statistically unlikely!) 'comics are not proper reading!'

Jake could feel another angry urge growing inside. He just couldn't understand why she kept saying this. It was obvious that comics *were* reading because they had *words* in them that you *read*! And anyway, graphic novels aren't comics, they're bigger and more complicated and better. She just refused to see it because they weren't about boring 'mum stuff', so she wouldn't even take the time to look at them.

Jake thought about not saying all this for a moment — he really did. But the urge got the better of him and, once again, angry words came spewing out of his mouth and everything turned into an argument and all he could think was that somehow his nice teatime had gone wrong and how it felt like the summer holidays were ruined before they had even begun.

'The bottom line is this Jake,' said Mum finally, after all the shouting had stopped and Sprat had run out of the open patio door into the garden to do a poo behind one of the gnomes. 'I'm taking you to the library tomorrow and we are going to choose some proper books for you to read this holiday and that's that.'

'Why doesn't Lucy have to do it?' Jake shot a sidelong glance at his sister, who so far, had done a good job of hiding behind the mayonnaise bottle.

'DON'T BRING ME INTO THIS YOU WORM!!'

Lucy went straight into screaming mode. Jake hated it when she did that, the sound made his brain hurt and it made her eyes bulge out of her head, which just looked ridiculous, 'JUST BECAUSE YOU ONLY EVER WANT TO READ THOSE STUPID COMICS! MUUUM! TELL HIM!'

As usual, Lucy had gone from zero to full nuclear in no time at all. It wasn't something she had always done, but ever since starting secondary school it was her new way of dealing with things. She would spend most of her time sullenly staring into her phone and grunting if anyone spoke to her. But the very instant that anything went wrong, she would explode into a white-hot rage that Jake had noticed was nearly always his fault somehow. It made him feel sad, like his lovely and kind big sister had gone away and been replaced by an evil robot sister from another dimension.

'STOP SHOUTING LUCY!' Mum shouted, which Jake found deeply ironic. 'Jake, Lucy doesn't have to do it because she's older than you and she has summer coursework to do and she actually reads proper books anyway. Now stop arguing and eat your beetroot instead of trying to hide it under the corned beef.'

And with that, Jake knew that all hope was lost and there was no escaping a boring trip to the library in his very near future.

2

The Boring Trip to the Library

'FIVE MINUTES! We're going in five minutes, make sure you brush your teeth!' Mum's voice echoed down the stairs. Jake, who had already brushed his teeth, because he always liked to brush his teeth *before* he ate breakfast, was busily shoving spoonful's of 'Captain Choco-Crunch' cereal into his mouth as fast as possible. It was the only cereal he would eat. Actually, it was the only *breakfast* he would eat, despite his mother's many attempts to bribe him with alternatives. Some of which were okay, but none of them had the perfect blend of chocolatey crunchiness and pleasant texture that the 'Captains' did. So, the back of the brightly coloured 'Captain Choco-Crunch' box had been Jake's breakfast table reading material for as long as he could remember. Sometimes there were awesome giveaways on the box, where you send away tokens for cool prizes, like a baseball cap, or a bowl that changed colour when you put the milk in, or best of all…the 'Captain Choco-Crunch Walkie Watches'. A pair of watches that were also walkie talkies (as long as they weren't too far apart!)

Before he could finish reading the comic strip on the back of the box for the twentieth time, Lucy burst into the room, snatched it off the table and waved it around above her head. Straight away Jake could feel an angry urge rising within him, he knew that if he didn't finish reading the strip, he would stay angry for the rest of the day. 'Hey!' he yelled through a mouthful of Choco-crunch, 'I'm reading that!' Lucy's face screwed up, making her look like a brussels sprout and Jake could tell that she was just about to say something mean about comics, when her phone suddenly beeped, and he was instantly forgotten. She dumped the box back on the table and stomped off with her thumbs frantically pummelling away at the tiny screen.

After breakfast, mum strapped Jake into the back of the family's trusty old blue camper van, which she insisted on calling the 'Dubster', and they set off through the winding streets of Bisby on their way to the library. It wasn't a long journey, there aren't really any long journeys in Bisby by the Sea, everywhere in Bisby is pretty close together. The only problem was, that the Dubster wasn't actually very good at going up hills, of which Bisby has many. Instead of just driving up the hills like every other car ever, it had a nasty habit of blowing out blue smoke and making loud grinding noises whenever faced with anything more than a very slight incline. And, although it would always get to the top in the end, the busy narrow streets and slow going meant that trips out in the Dubster could turn into awfully embarrassing experiences. Sometimes pedestrians would actually overtake them, squeezing their way past the slow moving, smoke belching machine as it wheezed its way up the hill. If they were local, they'd often take the time to wave a cheery hello, or even walk alongside for a casual chat through the window as the Dubster ponderously plodded up the hill. During the summer, when the streets were packed with tourists, people would stop and stare disapprovingly, or make a scene of squashing themselves into shop doorways, pulling their children close to them as their buckets and spades and rubber dinghies and lilos squeaked up against the windows. Today was one of those days, and the sight of all the happy families making their way to the beach just made Jake feel even more miserable.

'Nearly there love!' As usual, mum was blissfully oblivious to the chaos she was causing with the Dubster, but Jake knew better than to say anything. The beaten-up old van had belonged to dad. He had loved tinkering with it at the weekends and was always talking about doing it up and taking family trips in it. But he never got the chance to finish

The Dubster

it and the trips had never happened. After he died, mum couldn't bear to part with it and her job in a souvenir shop didn't pay very much, so she had sold her own car to pay for his funeral and the Dubster had become the only means the family had of getting around. Without dad working on it, the old van had started to fall apart a little bit more with each passing season, but it was as much a part of the family as Sprat or even Lucy, so it stayed.

With a splutter and a particularly loud **BANG!** the Dubster finally swung through a pair of imposing wrought-iron gates and into the carpark of the Bisby municipal

library. — Where it promptly died with a shudder and a cloud of blue smoke. 'Perfect timing!' announced mum cheerfully, grabbing dad's old shoebox full of emergency tools and clambering out.

Jake slid open the Dubster's door and stared up at the library, he had never actually noticed it before, despite knowing the town pretty well. It was an old building which, like most buildings in Bisby, was made from the local stone. The entrance was a large wooden door flanked by two scary looking lion statues, each clutching a thick book in its giant paws and peering down on those who dared to enter. There was something about their stony eyes that made Jake feel uneasy, but he knew they wouldn't eat him, because they were just statues and statues don't eat people, or at least not as far as he knew. A small, rusty plaque above the door announced that the library had been built in 1842 as the 'Bisby School For Errant Boys.' Jake decided that it didn't look very welcoming as either a school or a library. Even in the brilliant summer sunshine, its crumbling façade was hidden in gloomy shade.

'Here we are then,' said mum, shoving up her sleeves and opening the Dubster's creaky old engine cover. 'You go on inside and speak to Mrs Crisp the librarian, she'll tell you what to do. I'll be in as soon as I've found out what's upsetting the Dubster today.'

Jake had a pretty good idea what was upsetting the Dubster — it probably didn't like the library either! 'Fine,' he replied. 'But there'd better be some books about spaceships and robots and cool stuff and not just boring old ones about cowboys or whatever.'

'Muh-huh, okay cool, whatever, have fun.' said Mum. Her head was already buried deep in the Dubster's oily engine bay and she was hitting something with a hammer and muttering some words that Jake wasn't supposed to know.

After darting as fast as possible past the lions and through the wooden door, the first thing that Jake noticed about the library was the smell. It smelt of old people, cheap tea bags and rich tea biscuits. It was almost the exact same smell as Bisby church hall. He knew that because it was where mum had taken him to join the cub scouts, but he had only lasted for two weeks before the scout leader had said that he was 'too disruptive' and 'maybe he'd be happier somewhere else, like the Boy's Brigade.' The church hall was also where the children of Bisby all got taken to see Santa every Christmas, only it wasn't the real Santa, it was just Mr Pallet from the hardware store, who also smelt funny, like damp chipboard. But the smell in the library wasn't *exactly* the same as the church hall. There was something else about it, something more 'perfumey' and heavy. It made his head feel all heavy and swimmy, like when he span around too many times in the playground or stood up too quickly in the morning.

With every step, the old wooden floor creaked beneath his feet and dusty old chandeliers tinkled above his head. Blood red wallpaper with fuzzy patterns in dark maroon covered the walls. Each side of the corridor was lined with mouldy green lampshades with little golden tassels that dangled and spiralled around and around as though they were trying to hypnotise him. Music was playing from somewhere far away, it seemed to be coming from the floor above and trickling down through the knotholes in the wooden ceiling. It wasn't like any music he had heard before. Mum loved to put the radio on when she was cooking, but this didn't sound like that at all. For a start, there wasn't any words, it was just a strange, tinny, swirly sound that crackled and jumped and sounded more like it was coming out of a long tube than a speaker. It reminded him of the old Ferris wheel that he sometimes rode in on the seafront.

'Do you need something dear?'

The voice came from nowhere and made Jake jump out of his skin. (Not actually jump out of his skin, that would be gross! – Imagine the mess!)

Mrs Crisp

'I said do you need something dear?'

A tiny old woman had materialised in the hallway. Jake couldn't for the life of him work out where she had come from. She wasn't there before and then suddenly – *poof* — there she was.

'Erm,' he spluttered awkwardly, he hated talking to adults. 'My mum said she's signed me up for a summer reading competition or something.'

'Ah yes! You must be young Jake Starling then!' The hairs on the back of Jake's neck stood up, he hadn't expected the woman to know his name and it gave him the prickles. 'I'm Mrs Crisp, the librarian.' Her voice sounded like someone snapping a handful of dry twigs. 'Follow me, follow me, no time for dawdling Master Starling, summer won't last forever, the leaves will turn before you can blink.' The strange old lady turned on her heels and marched off at a surprisingly sprightly pace, leaving Jake trotting along behind her wondering what on earth was going on.

'My mum's just outside,' he called after her, 'she'll be in soon, she'll probably want to help me choose some books and … **OOF!**' The woman stopped so suddenly that Jake piled straight into the back of her. Strangely though, she didn't flinch, it was like colliding with a concrete wall.

'Master Starling.' She slowly turned to face him, it reminded Jake of an owl craning its head around to look for its prey. 'One does not simply 'choose' the books… it's the books that choose you.' Her eyes stayed fixed on his, peering over the top of her half-moon spectacles that barely clung to the end of her pointy nose. Jake let her words sink in for a moment before deciding that he had no idea at all what she meant. Confused and unsure of how to reply, he settled for just nodding and smiling. Dad had always told him that if he didn't understand what someone wanted from him, that just giving them a smile and a nod was always a good fall-back option. To be fair to dad, it actually worked pretty well. Mostly when he did it to people, they always seemed to leave him alone afterwards. But Mrs Crisp was still staring intently at him, it felt as though her watery blue eyes were peering straight into his brain and reading his every thought. He decided to test if she actually was and thought to himself, '*Hello? Can you hear me in here Mrs Crisp?*' There was no answer, but the strange smells were getting stronger and the weird music was getting even louder, and the tassels on the lights were twirling and whirling even faster and the dusty chandeliers were even more tinkly. He was just starting to feel a bit wobbly, when suddenly, the corridor started to stretch itself away behind Mrs Crisp, as though it was being dragged away from them, while they stayed standing still. It stretched out farther and farther away into the distance, an endless corridor filled with dancing lights and pungent smells.

'What sort of stories do you like Master Starling?'

Mrs Crisp's voice sounded as though it was coming from all around him, and Jake was sure that her lips hadn't moved at all when she spoke. Maybe she *was* in his head after all? It was getting hard to think with all the spinning lights and funny smells and the music, he was also pretty sure he was starting to hear animal sounds as well.

'Erm, I like graphic novels really, but mum says I have to read some proper books without pictures.' His reply sounded odd, like it had come from far away, and there were definitely animal sounds coming from somewhere. Perhaps someone was watching a documentary? It sounded like elephants and monkeys and parrots, definitely parrots — which seemed like an odd mix of animals.

'No pictures eh! Since when did pictures harm anyone I wonder?' Jake's heart pounded in his chest. The animal sounds had got even louder, and the smell had grown even headier, it hung over him like a thick blanket made of exotic perfume from a faraway land. 'Pictures have been telling stories for far longer than words Master Starling, your mother would do well to remember that.' She smiled and it looked as though her lips were moving in slow motion, her voice sounded all slow and deep, 'Tell me, have you ever seen one of these before?' Jake blinked, trying to fight away a sudden drowsiness that was threatening to overtake him. Mrs Crisp was holding a bizarre contraption in front of his face that she had produced from out of nowhere. It looked like an old-fashioned table lamp poking out of a cake tin full of tiny mirrors and faded old picture cards. 'It's called a '*praxinoscope*' Master Starling and it's a storyteller like no other – look inside, watch closely!' Jake lent over to peer inside and the praxinoscope started to spin. 'Lose yourself in its tales of wonder and mystery!' cackled Mrs Crisp, 'Lose yourself!'

The strange music swelled to a crescendo and the corridor faded away as the picture cards sprang to life, hurling themselves about in a chaotic dance. There were zebras and rhinos and men in suits with bowties and curious creatures that made no sort of sense at all. Women in flowing dresses and wrapped in feathers leapt and sidled and slinked through palm trees and pyramids, whilst the sun and moon took turns to rush overhead. Day turned into night and night turned into day over and over as stories of men and women and beings of all shapes and sizes danced around each other in a frenzy. Jake tried to look away, but he couldn't, it felt as though the praxinoscope was a tunnel, a peephole into a fantastical world that he should never have seen. A world that was luring him in. A world that existed so close and yet so far away, as though it was trapped just on the other side of a mirror on a dusty chest of drawers in a hidden room somewhere. The tiny figures beckoned to him, calling out his name. 'Come, come!' they called. 'Join us, join the dance!'

The corridor and Mrs Crisp had completely vanished, replaced by the silhouettes of hundreds of dancing figures. Somewhere, a clock began to tick. A steady *tick-tock, tick-tock*. Growing louder with every '*tick*' and louder still with every '*tock*', drowning out the music and the voices.

Tick-tock.

The sun replaced the moon one last time and its light chased away the silhouettes.

Tick-tock.

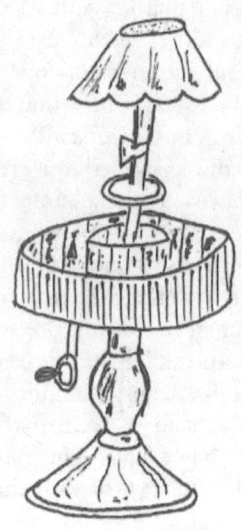

'And remember what I told you,' said Mrs Crisp. 'Those books are all we have left for the summer reading competition, and they are getting quite old now, so you must take care of them.'

'What?' Jake blinked, his head felt fuzzy and his

tongue tasted of sawdust, it felt as though he was waking from a dream.

'Don't say *'what'*, say *'pardon."* Jake was taken aback, Mrs Crisp sounded irritated, quite different to before, and the room was different too. The corridor with its creaky floor and tasselled wall lights had gone, there was no sign of the praxinoscope. He was standing in the middle of a large room, filled with shelves of musty smelling books, each wrapped in a wrinkled plastic dust cover and tagged with a number. An ancient computer sat on a beige steel trolley in one corner, a single red light blinking away on its equally beige casing. Next to it sat a torn off strip of worn looking stickers and a pile of dusty old floppy discs. 'I said, these are the last books that we have for the reading competition, and they are getting quite old, so you need to be careful with them. I'd advise you to always store them closed in a neat pile when you aren't reading them. Some people leave books lying around open and it bends the spine, which is a tragedy if you ask me.'

Jake nodded; he was more confused than he had ever been, 'Sorry Mrs Crisp, but what books are you talking about?' She looked at him as though he had just done a noisy smelly trump right there in the library. The same look that Miss Pillsbury gave him when he actually did do noisy smelly trumps in class.

'Those books! The books in your hands, the pile of books that I have just handed to you for the summer reading competition!'

Jake looked down and, sure enough, was surprised to find that he was clutching a pile of old and tatty looking books. Just as Mrs Crisp had said he was.

'Be sure to use a bookmark, and don't bend the pages back! It leaves big gaping gaps in the book and who knows what will happen if you make big gaping gaps in books. Books should be opened just enough to be read when one is reading, and nice and tightly closed when one is not. Books should always be stored properly on a bookshelf and given the respect that a good book deserves. Do you understand me Master Starling?'

Jake wasn't sure he understood her at all, he had no idea that books had so many rules! There certainly wasn't any of this fuss when he bought graphic novels off the internet. He didn't click 'buy it now' and then get a stern email warning him about using a bookmark and storing them nicely. Not to mention the fact that he had no idea how he had ended up in the library holding a pile of books he hadn't even seen before. The last thing he remembered was the smelly corridor and something about a table lamp and a cake tin? Or was there dancing? He had a vague recollection of something to do with dancing.

'Mrs Crisp,' he began, 'how did I…'

'There you are Jake! Hello Mrs Crisp, how are you?' Mum came bustling into the library still clutching dad's old hammer and smothered in engine oil. 'Oh fantastic, you've chosen some books. Thank you so much Mrs Crisp, I hope he wasn't any trouble. Come on Jake I've got the Dubster going, but I didn't dare turn her off so she's in the car park with the engine running, which means we've really got to dash. Sorry Mrs Crisp and thank you, we'll get these books back to you all ticked off and read by the end of the holidays. Have a lovely day! Come on Jake, *wake up!*' With that mum ushered Jake out of the library, down the smelly corridor, past the lions and back into the bustle of Bisby and the warmth of the midday sun.

3

Three Books, One Genius and Dippy Eggs

WHEN THEY GOT HOME, Jake hurtled up the stairs as fast as his legs would carry him. He dashed into his room, slammed the door shut and threw the pile of books on the bed. 'Are you okay dear?' mum called up the stairs. 'You didn't say a word all the way back.'

'I'm fine!' Jake called down. 'I'm just…erm… keen to get reading!' He wasn't at all keen to get reading, but he knew it was what mum wanted to hear and it would buy him some time to think about what had just happened.

'Okay, but don't overdo it and give yourself a headache.'

'Sure, okay, I won't.' Jake eyed the books; he just couldn't understand how they had come to be in his hands. He didn't remember choosing them at all, and from the looks of them, they weren't the type of books he would have picked in a million years. Or even a billion, or even a zillion! He cautiously picked up the first book and ran his hands over the wrinkled see through protector. Underneath, the cover was faded, as though the book had sat in a shop window for years. The picture on the front was of a blonde boy wearing a chunky knit, pale blue turtleneck jumper. He was holding his hands up to his ruddy cheeks, with a badly drawn expression of fear on his face. Behind him loomed a skinny creature dressed in rags with pale green skin, long greasy hair and a knobbly wooden club clutched in its bony fingers. The title of the book was written in a cheesy font that Jake presumed was meant to look scary, it was called 'The Curse of the Bog Troll' by Reginald Ochre. A quick flip through revealed that there were a few pictures dotted throughout the book. Not the beautifully drawn, action packed scenes like in his graphic novels, but simple line sketches that looked like they had been thrown together as an afterthought. He gave a *harrumph* and tossed the book aside, it landed in a heap somewhere in his smelly pants and socks corner. He didn't bother to check where.

Next he turned his attention to the second book. It was even more faded than the first one, and it smelt funny, like old cheese, (although that may have been the smell coming from his stinky socks!) The cover had a picture of an old-fashioned explorer on the front. He was wearing a tan coloured pith helmet and khakis and clutching a large hunting rifle as he heroically faced down a charging rhinoceros. The title of the book was 'Jungle Adventure', which Jake decided was the single worst title for a book he had ever heard. The author's name was 'Archibald Montgomery', which sounded exactly like the sort of name you would expect for the author of a book about a jungle adventure. A quick scan through the pages revealed a few simple pictures here and there, and far too many words to be bothered with. Even without reading it, Jake decided that it was probably the most boring book ever written. Out of curiosity, he jumped straight to the back page to see how the most boring book ever written ended, after all it wasn't as if he was actually going to read it. But if he knew how it ended it would be far easier to convince mum that he had!

> *'Captain Smith flashed his gallant smile once more and stubbed out his cigar with such vim and vigour, that the embers blazed before him, giving him the appearance of a fiery being from another realm. 'And with that sirs, I bid you farewell!' Smith tucked the beast's mighty horn into his belt and strode forth from the smoking room, leaving nought but befuddlement and awe in his wake. For he had proven his boast, as he had promised he would. Captain Smith, truly was the greatest hunter in all of England.'*

Reading this actually made Jake snort with laughter so much that a large bubble of snot came out his nose and plopped right onto the book, where it stayed when he slammed it shut and propelled it over his shoulder to land somewhere in a pile of old toys.

'Go on then, let's see what number three has to offer,' he chuckled to himself. Book number three was bigger than the other two, and its plastic dust covering had melted away on one corner where someone had probably left it too close to something hot, like a candle or a heater, or a volcano or an angry dragon. (The last two are probably unlikely, but you never know!) The front cover had a picture of an unusual creature that Jake had never seen before. It looked a bit like a dark brown potato or a chunky poo (a poo-tato?) with skinny arms and legs and a mean, wizened face that scowled out at him from behind the wrinkly, melted dust cover. Something about the picture gave Jake the creeps, it seemed as though the creature's piggy, marbly little eyes were looking straight at him. As an experiment, he turned his head, first to the left, and then to the right. Yes! The eyes really did seem to follow him. He tried keeping his head still and turning the book, first to the left, and then to the right, and the exact same thing happened. There was no doubt about it, the creature was definitely looking back at him. '*That's clever,*' he thought, and quickly flipped through the pages. The book was called 'The Nefarious Glub' by Meredith Quandary. As far as he could tell, the story was all about a large family of brothers and sisters who encounter a nefarious creature called the 'Glub' and ended up chasing it around for some reason or another. Either way, it looked boring and old and the picture was creepy. Jake was just about to hurl it over his shoulder when he realised that his plan to read just the back pages was a stroke of actual genius, and if he did it for all three books, he might be able to fool mum into thinking that he had actually read them all. So, he quickly flipped to the end and this, dear reader, is what he found there.

> *'And even though they never stopped looking, even when their children's children had grown up, none of the family ever saw the Glub again. It was as though he had never even existed at all, but of course, they knew that truly he had. And that was enough.'*

Jake was just thinking what a cop-out, rubbish ending that was when he realised that he had forgotten to sneak a peek at the ending of 'The curse of the Bog Troll' before propelling it across the room. He was about to hunt for it, when mum's voice wafted up the stairs. 'Dinner's ready love, it's dippy egg and soldiers!' The moment he heard the words *dippy egg and soldiers*, Jake tossed the book over his head and dashed out the door and was halfway down the stairs before it had landed.

4

The Fancy Pasty

THE NEXT DAY was Lucy's birthday, which meant a trip to the beach with half a dozen of Lucy's annoying friends, followed by descending en masse on The Fancy Pasty for lunch. The Fancy Pasty was the very best pasty shop in all of Bisby by the Sea, with a mind-boggling selection of pastys to choose from. Mum always said The Fancy Pasty was the main reason that dad had wanted to move to Bisby in the first place, back when Lucy was still a bump and not a grump.

Beryl Broom

The owner of The Fancy Pasty was an extremely

rotund lady called Beryl Broom who always wore a large white apron with a picture of a pasty on it around her middle, and big round glasses that made her eyeballs look huge. Her bright white hair was always tied up in a giant bun on top of her head and Dad had once said she looked like the 'Michelin Man'. Afterwards, mum had poked him in the ribs and done a *tutsigh* at him. The memory made Jake smile and he made a mental note to find out who the Michelin Man was when he got home.

'Happy Birthday Lucy!' sang Mrs Broom, clearing a space in the middle of the table and plonking down the biggest and most bonkers pasty Jake had ever seen. Instead of being filled with meat and vegetables, it was packed with marshmallows, fizzy sweets and popping candy and it had fourteen candles sticking out the top. The twisty crust was striped like a candy cane and the whole thing was slathered in squirty cream and lay on a bed of rapidly melting smarties. 'Here you go, one 'birthday special', tuck in girls!' The gaggle of noisy girls didn't need telling twice and they started devouring the vast pasty in a frenzied flurry of plastic forks.

Mrs Broom smiled down at Jake, 'Don't worry love, I've got a special treat just for you too. Here you go, a 'Meat 'n Sweet' with no crust and served on a plain plate. Just how you like it.' She gave Jake and his mum a warm smile and made her way back to the kitchen, whilst cheerfully wiggling her bottom along to the 'Spice Girls' song playing on the radio.

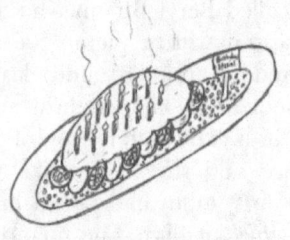

Just as Jake was tucking into the meaty end of the 'Meat 'n Sweet', mum's phone started vibrating with that awful *BWAAAH* sound that phones make when they vibrate on a wooden table. *BWAAAH* went the phone, *BWAAAH*. After the third *BWAAAH*, mum finally managed to choke down her mouthful of pasty enough to answer it. Jake recognised the picture on the screen straight away, it was Rita, his best friend Ajay's mum. Jake listened intently to the call, whilst trying not to show that he was listening intently, because mum had said that it was rude to listen to other people's phone calls — even if they are sat right next to you and the phone call is about you. This was something he had found out after Miss Pillsbury had called home once to explain to mum about how he had hidden under her desk and refused to come out for the entire afternoon, because someone had accidentally knocked an entire bowl of disgusting pink custard all over him in the dinner hall.

After a few moments, mum put her hand over the phone's mouthpiece. She turned to him and said, 'Ajay's mum has to go away for a few days because her brother Harish lives in London and he isn't feeling very well. She wants to know if Ajay can stay with us while she goes to visit him. It's okay with me, but he'll have to share a room with you. Do you think that will be alright?'

Before Jake could answer, Lucy piped up at full volume, 'MUUUUM!' she shrieked, spraying bits of chewed up candy-striped pasty all over the table. 'THAT'S NOT FAIR! WHY DOES *HE* GET A SLEEP OVER ON *MY* BIRTHDAY?' Mum shot her an evil look that silenced her in no time at all.

'Yes, that's alright,' Jake muttered. He was more concerned about how close Lucy's spray had got to his lovely Meat 'n Sweet pasty. The thought of it being covered in sister spray suddenly made it seem a lot less appetising.

'Good, that's sorted then,' mum turned back to her phone. 'Hello Rita, yes, he's very excited.... yes.... any time after six.... yes.... a toothbrush....no.... clean pants.... yes.... spare key.... of course. Okay. I do hope everything's alright with Harish. Do keep me posted, won't you...lovely, see you later...ciao...ciao...bye!'

Jake did a special inside-his-head smile. He loved hanging out with Ajay, and in all the excitement of birthdays and sleepovers, it looked as though mum had totally forgotten about the stupid, smelly book reading competition thing. Maybe this summer *was* going to be alright after all!

The rest of Lucy's birthday passed by in a blur of over-the-top shrieking, far-too-loud party poppers, making pointless videos, taking stupid selfies and unwrapping presents. Jake stayed well out of the girls' way and spent the afternoon carefully moving things around in his room to make space for the old camp bed that Ajay would sleep on. At 6:05 precisely, the doorbell rang, and a harassed looking Rita shoved Ajay through the door, handed mum his bag and gave her a grateful hug before driving off in a shower of gravel. Jake watched her go with great admiration, she had a red Mazda MX-5 sports car that was so much cooler than the Dubster. She'd taken him out in it once and it was epic, and he was definitely going to buy one when he was old enough to drive. Or a Toyota MR-2, they were cool too.

'Why don't you take Ajay upstairs and get settled in, I'll bring you up some popcorn later if you like,' said Mum. That sounded like a great plan, so the two boys headed up to Jake's room.

'What's wrong with your uncle?' asked Jake, handing Ajay a controller and turning on his games console. 'Is he going to die?'

Ajay thought carefully for a moment before replying, he and Jake had been best friends since they were both bumps in their mum's tummies, so he was well used to the way that Jake could sometimes seem rude when he didn't mean to be. 'I don't think so,' he replied eventually. 'Mum didn't say much about it, but she did cry a bit.'

A few hours later, the summer sun streaming in through the bedroom window had turned to a brilliant red twilight, and the distant sounds of the boats *clonking* in the harbour drifted in on the evening breeze. Both the controllers needed recharging and the boys had finally grown bored of games. 'Do you want to watch 'Mecha-Dawn'?' asked Jake.

Ajay knew it was only a matter of time before Jake suggested they watch 'Mecha-Dawn', it was his favourite film and they had watched it together at least twenty times, and, while Ajay loved it too, if he was honest he *was* starting to get a bit bored of watching the same giant robots punch the same gigantic lizards in the face *every* time he visited. But he never had the heart to say 'no', so instead he nodded his head and smiled and said, 'Sure, let's do that.'

Feeling very pleased that Ajay had agreed, Jake rummaged around under the television in

search of the disc, but it wasn't there, which was odd, because it was always there, because that was where he kept it.

'Maybe you moved it somewhere when you were getting the bed out for me?' suggested Ajay, seeing the look of panic and confusion on his friend's face.

'No, I didn't, why would I move a disc that's under the telly to make room for a bed? The bed's not under the telly is it!' Jake retorted. He could feel himself starting to get upset, he hated it when things weren't where they were supposed to be, and an irritated urge was already starting to rise up inside him.

'Tell you what,' said Ajay. 'Let's move some stuff around and see if it shows up. That nearly always works for me, and then if we still can't find it, we'll ask your mum to help. Mums can always find everything that's missing, it's like their superpower!' Jake considered this for a moment. It seemed like an absurd idea, after all, what was the point of looking anywhere other than right where the disc was supposed to be? *But*, if it wasn't right where it was supposed to be, then that must mean that it *had* to be somewhere else, however unlikely.

'Fine,' he conceded, after thoroughly thinking it through. 'Let's move some stuff.'

The two friends started working their way around Jake's room, peering under things, peeping into things and lifting things up. But the disc was nowhere to be found.

'Hey, what's the deal with this weird book?' Ajay had bravely stuck a hand under Jake's clothes pile and was holding up the copy of 'The Nefarious Glub'. He was looking at it like it might as well have been one of Jake's stinky socks. The sight of the book brought all the memories rushing back to Jake. He had completely forgotten to tell his friend about the library and the weird old lady and the rubbish books he had ended up with. But before he could explain what had happened, Ajay turned the book around and pointed at the front cover with a confused expression on his face. "I mean, why's the cover just blank, that's a bit weird isn't it?'

It took Jake a few seconds to process what he was seeing. Ajay was there, the book was there, the *title* of the book was there. But the picture on the front of the book, the picture of the odd brown creature that looked a bit like a potato or a poo (Poo-tato!) was just…gone. There was nothing left at all, just a plain background, the author's name and the title. That was it. No sign of 'The Nefarious Glub' anywhere.

Jake snatched the book out of Ajay's hands and studied it closely.

'Hey, sorry I didn't mean to…' Ajay's voice faded away when he saw the look on Jake's face. He had turned a deathly shade of pale and was frantically turning the book over and over and peering inside it. At one point, he lifted it above his head and started vigorously shaking it, as though he expected something might fall out. Then, without saying a word, Jake shoved the book back into Ajay's hands, pushed him aside and dived headfirst into the clothes pile sending socks and pants flying everywhere. He was like a dog digging for a bone! At one point, a particularly stinky sock hit Ajay right in the eye, and a pair of blue superhero pants *plopped* onto his head. But he didn't complain, he was too busy worrying that Jake's brain had gone wrong, like that time when the ancient old cassette tape player at school had gone all wobbly, and brown tape had come flying out all over the place, and the French teacher had started shouting, 'ZUT ALORS! MON VIEUX TRICOLORE!' and frantically started doing something odd with the broken

cassette tape and a pencil.

He really hoped that brown tape wasn't going to

start spewing out of Jake's ears or anything weird like that.

Oh, dear reader, little did Ajay know, that things most certainly *were* about to get weird. Things were about to get *very* weird indeed!

After a few minutes of rummaging, Jake suddenly let out a loud 'AH HA!' and emerged from the pile, triumphantly clutching two more books. Both of which had front covers that were as blank as 'The Nefarious Glub'. No, that's not quite true — They weren't quite blank. One had a forlorn looking man sitting on a pith helmet all alone in a jungle, but behind him was a big empty space where a rhino had been. The other book also had a big, empty space, and what looked like the top of a blonde head right at the very bottom, as though someone was trying to hide but hadn't ducked down quite far enough. But of the bog troll, there was no sign. Jake opened first one book and then the other, frantically flipping back and forth through the pages.

The Fancy Pasty

'Jake,' said Ajay quietly and in his most calming voice. 'Is everything…alright?'

Jake stared at him for a long moment, his big brown eyes were open wider than Ajay had ever seen them before, when he spoke, his voice was little more than a whisper. 'No,' he gulped, 'I think we may have a problem!"

5

A Strange Encounter

'SO, LET ME GET THIS STRAIGHT,' said Ajay. 'You're seriously telling me that you think you might've somehow accidentally borrowed some magic books from the Bisby library?' He had listened quietly while Jake had told him all about his strange experience with Mrs Crisp and her weird praxinoscope, but he just couldn't hold down his disbelief any longer.

'Yes,' replied Jake.

'And you're sure they're not just blank notebooks or something?'

'Yes, I'm sure! Mrs Crisp told me not to leave the books open or with the pages turned back. Ajay, I think she knew this might happen! I probably should have paid more attention to what she was saying.' Ajay could tell that Jake was getting really stressed out, because his cheeks had started turning pink. 'They had words in them before, I know they did because I read them, but they've just… gone!'

'Words don't just disappear from books Jake.'

'YES, I KNOW! BUT THEY HAVE! AND SO HAVE THE PICTURES ON THE FRONT!' Jake had become somewhat animated.

'Is everything alright in here boys?' Jake's mum

appeared at the door clutching a bowl of popcorn, her face suggested that she knew full well that everything was not 'alright'.

'YEESS!!' chorused the boys in their most innocent voices. Jake's mum's eyes travelled around the room suspiciously, taking in every minute detail as only a mum's eyes can. 'Okay then,' she was clearly unconvinced. 'Let me know soon if you need anything else, because I'm going to take some tablets and head off to bed. All the screaming today has given me one of my headaches, so don't stay awake all night chatting okay!'

'Okay, night mum,' nodded Jake.

'Night Mrs Starling,' nodded Ajay.

Jake's mum rubbed at her temples and backed out of the room leaving the boys to breathe a sigh of relief. If she was still suspicious, at least her headache would be a useful distraction while they worked out what they were going to do about their mysterious book problem.

When he was sure she had gone, Ajay turned to Jake, 'Look, let's say I believe you and we really do have three magical book creatures on the loose, what exactly are we supposed to do about it?' Jake pondered this for a moment, he put his fingers on his chin to help him think and made a '*hmm*' sound. It was something that always worked in graphic novels and on TV, so it had to be worth a try.

'Well,' he said after a moment. 'I suppose we'll have to go looking for them, I mean, they can't have gone far. Let's start by splitting up and hunting around the house. We can use my Captain Choco-Crunch walkie-watches to stay in touch.' Without wasting a moment, Jake reached into his bedside drawer and pulled out a pair of chocolate coloured walkie watches and a couple of small LED torches that he had got from last year's Christmas crackers. He handed Ajay one of each, 'Here take a torch and put this on, we'll have to sneak because mum and Lucy won't be asleep just yet. You start with the upstairs and I'll start in the cellar and we'll meet in the living room, stay in touch.'

'Right,' Ajay nodded confidently. 'So — just to be clear — I'm looking for a skinny green troll, a rhino and a 'Glub', which is a creature that looks a bit like a poo or a potato with arms and legs?'

'Yes,' Jake replied earnestly. 'A poo-tato, but I can't imagine that the rhino is a full-size rhino, otherwise my room would be a total disaster, and I doubt it would've got down the stairs.' Ajay had to admit that he had a point.

'Right, so a troll, a poo and a very small rhino then, got it! Good luck!' He started towards the bedroom door, before spinning on his heels so fast that it made Jake jump. 'Hang on a minute, what do we do if we actually find one? I mean, how are we supposed to get it back in the book?'

'You know, I hadn't thought of that...*hmmm*.' The two boys pondered some more for a minute, until Jake suddenly yelped, 'I've got it!' He dashed over to his wardrobe, flung open the door and rummaged around for a moment.

Jake had a habit of being *really* into something for a while and then suddenly deciding it was boring and chucking it all into the wardrobe before getting *really* into something else.

One by one, he started throwing things out onto the bedroom floor. First to come out was his old roller skates, then a keyboard. Next was a pogo stick and a large box of flags. A model train set appeared after that, and a magician's

hat, quickly followed by a science experiment set. Finally, after a particularly big *heave*, he emerged from the very deepest, darkest depths of the wardrobe, triumphantly clutching two unusually large fishing nets. 'Here,' he panted. 'We can use these, but I'll have the green one because it was dads.'

Ajay took the other net and the two boys tip-toed their way out onto the landing, where luckily the carpet was super soft and squishy, making it easy to sneak. The only rooms upstairs were the bedrooms, which were all occupied with their doors shut tight, the small bathroom and Mrs Starling's study where she kept all of her unfinished art projects. Ajay decided that barging into either Mrs Starling's or Lucy's bedroom was probably a terrible idea, so he decided to start with the study. Jake gave him a wave and made his way down the stairs, making sure not to tread on any of the creaky steps.

The door to the study was ajar just enough for Ajay to poke his head around, so he flicked on the torch and aimed the beam through the gap. Nothing leapt out at him, which he considered to be a good start, but it didn't mean that it was all clear. The only way to be truly sure was to go inside. His mind was racing almost as fast as his heart, he had never hunted anything before, let alone escaped book characters, and he wasn't entirely clear on what he was supposed to do if he did find anything. 'Hello,' he whispered. 'Is anyone in here?' The only sounds were the faraway *clonking* of the boats in the harbour and the gentle *swish* of the waves drifting in through the open window. He held his breath for a moment, the net gripped so tightly in his hands that his knuckles started to turn white. Mrs Starling's artwork looked super strange in the eerie torchlight. Mostly it was paintings of boats and beach huts, but there were also some mirrors with driftwood frames which caught the torchlight, making Ajay jump at his own reflection. Feeling a bit silly, he decided to prove to himself how brave he was really and stepped even further into the room. He swept the torch around looking for any sign of something unusual and the beam fell across a selection of knee-high stuffed animals. There was a flowery pink giraffe, a bright red parrot, a yellow teddy and a rhino wearing a big floppy hat. But there was no sign of any escaped book creatures. With a sigh he decided to leave the study and check in the bathroom instead.

He was halfway out the door before the penny dropped!

The Book-Rhino

In a flash, he whirled the torch around, pointed it straight at the rhino and whispered, 'AH HA! GOTCHA!' in his most ferocious whisper.

. . .

A Strange Encounter

The floppy hat was still there, but there was no sign of the rhino that just had been underneath it! Ajay's heart skipped a beat, 'Oh no!' The book-rhino *was* real! Trying to be as quiet as possible, he crept back into the room with the net at the ready.

A grey blur flashed in the corner of his eye, and he gave the net a mighty *swish*, but caught nothing but air. 'Jake,' he whispered into the watch, 'Jake, its Ajay, you won't believe this, I've found the rhi...' Before he could finish his sentence, the small, grey book-rhino leapt down from its hiding place in Mrs Starling's vintage lampshade and landed straight on top of his head with a meaty *plop*! Ajay desperately wanted to scream, but he knew if he did, that Mrs Starling and Lucy would wake up and the game would be up! He would have to explain why he was in their art room in the middle of the night waving an old fishing net around. And then he'd have to try to convince them about the missing book creatures — by which time, the creatures could be anywhere and up to who-knows-what! So instead of screaming, he made a strange '*tzzzzztzzzztzzz*' sound and flapped his arms around above his head in an attempt to bat away the book-rhino like it was a very large wasp. Which worked, sort of.

The book-rhino deftly ducked and dived and hopped from one leg to the other to avoid Ajay's flailing arms. It ended up doing a fancy little rhino-dance on Ajay's head before losing its footing, sliding down his face and landing in his lap, where it sat for a moment, looking quite bewildered. Wasting no time at all, Ajay grabbed the net and *swished* it up high, ready to *swoosh* it down onto the book-rhino as hard as he could manage.

Only it didn't *swoosh*.

It just sort of...stayed there, stuck in the air above his head. Confused, Ajay sneaked a peak up to see what the net had got stuck on, but the very second his eyes flicked upwards, the book-rhino saw its chance, and made a dash for the open window as fast as its stubby little legs could carry it.

'No!' Ajay let out a strangled half-whisper-half-cry.

'*Hee hee*, too bad little boy, the rhino's gone and escaped your ploy!'

A bizarre, sing-song voice came from above Ajay's head where an odd little potatoey looking creature was dangling from the vintage lampshade by its feet and holding on to the net with its spindly arms.

'And now I shall beat my swift retreat, until again the Glub you meet!' it crowed, obviously feeling very pleased with itself. And with that, the awful creature wrinkled up its nose, stuck out its small purple tongue and hurled itself through the air in a quite impressive loop-the-loop, before landing on the windowsill. Once there, it blew a very noisy and very wet raspberry, before turning around and jumping straight out the window after the rhino.

Ajay scrambled to his feet, his face turning an unusually bright shade of red. He dashed to the window and peered down at the Starling's lawn below, where he saw the most bizarre sight he had ever seen. The Glub was riding the book-rhino like a horse, with one of his wiry arms held aloft as though leading a charge. Ajay hissed down at them, 'Stop, wait!' But it was too late, the extraordinary pair of creatures dashed across the moonlit lawn, shot down the garden path, leapt neatly over the gate and vanished into the darkness of the warm Bisby night.

6

An Even Stranger Encounter

THINGS HAD GONE RATHER...*DIFFERENTLY* for Jake.

He had just been heading down to the cellar to begin his own book-creature-hunt, when he had been overwhelmed with a sudden desire to answer a call of nature. (Which is a very polite way of saying that he needed a wee!) He was just about to open the door to the big downstairs bathroom, when he heard a strange sound coming from inside. Now, strange sounds coming from bathrooms isn't in itself an entirely unusual occurrence. Jake himself had a made a few odd toilet noises in the past. But this didn't sound like *that* sort of noise, and anyway, everybody else was upstairs. So that meant that whoever — or whatever — was making the unpleasant sounds in the bathroom, was something that wasn't supposed to be there — something like a creature that had escaped from a magical book.

Jake steeled himself by imagining that he was one of the giant robots from 'Mecha-Dawn' about to confront a giant space lizard. He counted to three inside his head, raised his dad's old green net above his head, and flung open the door as suddenly as he could.

An Even Stranger Encounter

What he found inside was not what he had expected!

It was the bog troll. That much was evident, it looked exactly as it had done when it had been in its proper place — on the front cover of 'The Curse of the Bog Troll' book. Its skin was green, its hair was long and greasy, and its fingers were bony. Thankfully, it wasn't holding a club. '*The club must've stayed in the book, luckily for me!*' thought Jake, staring at the creature.

The unexpected part was not that the bog troll was in the toilet.

It was that the bog troll was *in the toilet*. Like, actually *in* the toilet.

In Jake's life there had been many times when he had chosen not to speak, but there hadn't been many where he had found himself completely and utterly speech*less*. But that is precisely what happened when he found the bog troll standing — yes, *standing* with both of its feet wedged firmly in the toilet and chewing — yes, *chewing* on the toilet brush! A thin dribble of vile brown water ran down its chin and stained its ragged vest and Jake was sure that he would throw up then and there, but he couldn't...because the toilet was blocked...by a bog troll!

'Oh hey,' said the disgusting creature through a mouthful of bristles and second-hand loo roll. 'Sorry man, did you want some?' Jake stared in horror as the creature pulled the brush from its mouth with a wet squelch and offered him the dripping, chewed up mass of unspeakable grossness. 'It's really good, the chrome handle makes the whole experience just that bit more classy than your 'bog standard' brush, if you'll pardon the pun! Get it... '*Bog standard*?'

Jake was still staring at the creature; his brain hadn't yet managed to persuade his mouth to speak.

'Nah? Not funny? Ok,

fair enough, sorry man, it's a bog troll thing. My name's Keith by the way, Keith the bog troll. Sorry if I'm holding up the proceedings, I'll just finish up here and then I'll be out of your way.'

Jake finally remembered how to speak, and hissed, 'STOP!' as loudly as he dared.

The bog troll paused mid-chomp and rolled its yellow eyes towards him.

'Oh, sorry, were you saving this? My bad, here you go fella, there's still some juicy bits left,' It held the chewed-up toilet brush out in one of its grisly hands.

'No, you should stop because it's *very, very poisonous*!' said Jake in his sternest voice.

'Really?' replied the bog troll, looking horrified. 'What sort of villain would poison a man's snack? Oh my gosh, you saved me! You're my hero, thanks pal. Hey, I didn't catch your name.'

'My name is Jake,' Jake folded his arms to show that he meant business. (It was a trick he'd picked up from mum.) 'And it's not 'been poisoned'— it's a toilet brush! They're not supposed to be eaten, *because they're for cleaning toilets*. THEY'RE POISONOUS BECAUSE THEY'RE COVERED IN GERMS!'

(Dearest reader, Jake was and is entirely and utterly correct about this, they most certainly are *very* germy indeed and are best left to grown-ups.)

. . .

'Well they aren't poisonous to bog trolls,' retorted Keith in a very grumpy voice. 'They're tasty.'

'I don't care!' replied Jake. Mum says they are germy and not to touch them and this is mum's house, so we follow mum's rules. Got it!'

Keith the bog troll considered this for a moment, until eventually, he shuffled around awkwardly in the toilet bowl and placed the mangled, chewed-up toilet brush back in its holder.

KEITH - The Bog-Troll

'Thank-you,' said Jake. 'Now would you mind explaining why you are standing in my downstairs toilet and aren't upstairs in the book *where you belong*?' Keith looked like he was about to cry, his skinny lips started to tremble, and his bloodshot yellow eyes started to well up. A single brown tear slid down his pale green cheek.

'Oh dude, I'm sorry,' he choked. 'It just gets really boring in there after a while, living the same old story over and over. So, when a chance to escape came along I just sort of, took it, y'know? I mean, it only happens once in like every…' The creature paused and started counting on its bony digits before giving up, '…every now and then.' Jake tried not to barf from the smell of the creature's breath and nodded a serious nod, Keith's story made perfect sense. 'When you threw the book away, it landed open, so I managed to pop myself out. I was having a little look around the place and then you all came home, so I hid in the cistern until it all went quiet. I was just about to flush myself away on a bit of an explore to see what's what, when I spotted this particularly tasty looking loo brush and, well, you know the rest.'

'I see,' said Jake. 'And what about the others?'

Keith gave him a blank stare, 'What others dude?'

'The other book creatures, the rhino and the Glub, where are they?' Just as he had asked the question, Jake's walkie watch sprang to life with a *crackle*, and Ajay's voice wafted from the tiny speaker, '*Jake, Jake its Ajay, you won't believe this, I've found the rhi…*'

Jake and the bog troll stared at each other for a moment.

'Oh,' said Keith. '*Those* others. Yeah, those guys suck, I dunno where they are.' He pointed at the walkie watch, 'But it sounds like that guy does, he sounds nice, maybe you should ask him.'

'That's my best friend Ajay. Come on, I'm going to help him and you're coming with me — but you have to be quiet because mum's asleep, okay. And try not to breathe on me, you have very stinky breath!'

The bog troll looked longingly at the flush handle for a moment, and then looked back at Jake, and then back at the flush handle, and then back at Jake. 'Alright fine,' he sighed. 'But once I've helped, *then* can I go explore?'

'You explore by flushing yourself down the toilet?' asked Jake, who so far had surprised himself with how calm he had remained throughout the whole bizarre conversation.

'Yeah,' Keith seemed surprised that Jake didn't know this. 'It's how we bog trolls get around, we flush ourselves down the bog and *whoosh* around through the pipes, the clue's sort of in the name.'

Jake eyed the bog troll up and down, it wasn't as big as it had looked on the cover of the book, in fact, it wasn't much taller than he was, but it was definitely too big to fit round a U-bend. 'But how do you fit?'

Keith raised one spiky eyebrow at Jake, 'Dude, I came out of a magic book.'

'Fair point,' said Jake. 'Come on.'

7

A Band in Ship

JAKE and the bog troll had made it as far as the kitchen when they bumped straight into a scared looking Ajay — who took one look at the freaky green creature standing behind Jake and let out a strangled *squeak!* He shoved Jake aside and hurled his net straight at the scary-looking creature's face, smacking it square in the nose.

'OW! Dude, did you just *throw* a net at me?' Keith the bog troll clutched at his pointy nose with tears streaming down his cheeks. 'That *really* hurt man! You do know that's not even how you use a net right? Look, you've gone and made my eyes water! And before you say it, NO, I'm not crying! My eyes are just *watering* because you hit my nose when you *threw* a net at me! I mean, who *throws* a net for goodness sake?'

'Ajay, this is Keith the bog troll, Keith the bog troll, this is my best friend Ajay,' whispered Jake, trying not to laugh. 'And could you both please remember to keep the noise down, or mum and Lucy will wake up and then we'll really be in trouble.'

Ajay's mouth was opening and closing like a goldfish that's been taken out of its fish tank, or pond, or little plastic bag, or whatever you keep your goldfish in.

'Hey Ajay, good to meet you, '*Mr I throw nets at people I've only just met.*' Keith the bog troll let go of his nose, wiped his eyes and offered Ajay a scrawny hand. Ajay was just about to shake it when Jake stopped him.

'Actually mate, I probably wouldn't do that! Let's just say I know where that hand's been!' He gave his friend a knowing look, and all three of them stared at Keith's slightly drippy hand for a moment. 'So, what happened upstairs?' asked Jake. 'Did you see anything?'

Jake and Keith listened carefully whilst Ajay described his run in with the book-rhino and the nefarious Glub. Once he had finished, Keith shook his head with a pained expression on his face. 'I knew something like this would happen eventually,' he moaned. 'That Glub has always been trouble, leading other book characters astray and getting into mischief, they don't call him nefarious for nothing! There was this one time, he escaped from his book and managed to find his way onstage at a band concert. He was dancing around behind the singer for at least five minutes. All the girls were pointing and screaming, but the singer just thought they were screaming for him! They were a pretty good band too, 'The Beatles' I think they were called. They'll probably go far one day.'

Jake rubbed the top of his head; too many stressful thoughts were starting to build up inside. He knew that if they didn't get the creatures back into the books by morning, they might be spotted, and then who knows *what* might happen. Perhaps the government would come to Bisby in white suits with helmets and catch the magical book creatures with helicopters and stun guns and lock them up or something. And even worse, if they found out where the book creatures had come from, they might take him and Ajay away and lock them up and do experiments on them too! — Which wasn't a very nice thought.

'We need to get out of here and start looking for the Glub and the rhino quickly,' he said. 'We have to find them before morning, or the government might come and lock us all up and do experiments on us!'

'I have no idea what a government is, but you seem pretty smart, so I'm sure you're probably right,' nodded Keith.

The three of them sneaked out of the back door and into the night. The sun had finally slipped below the horizon leaving just the faintest smudge of red visible in the west and the moon was already shining brightly in the sky. Even though it was still warm, Jake felt a shiver run through him. He wasn't sure if it was excitement, or a little bit of fear at going out at night without mum. He had never been out so late before, let alone running around Bisby with a stinky bog troll looking for escaped magical creatures.

'Where's the nearest place where there might be lots of people?' asked Keith.

Jake thought for a moment, 'Well, at this time of night, it's probably down in 'The Ship'.

'Right, we'll start there then.'

The Ship Inn was the busiest pub and restaurant in Bisby. Jake had been there lots of times before, for scampi in a basket and a bottle of fizzy pop with mum and Lucy, and even with dad when he was still alive. 'But children aren't allowed in The Ship without a grown-up,' Ajay protested. He gave Keith a sidelong glance, 'And I don't think they let bog trolls in at all.'

'Outrageous!' gasped Keith, clutching a hand to his chest. 'In this day and age! That's prejudice that is! That's exclusion on the basis of bog-trollery! I feel wounded, I feel targeted, my inner child is weeping! Why can't I just be accepted for who I am? Oh mercy-me!'

Jake and Ajay didn't really know what to say to all that, so they just stood back and watched while Keith threw himself onto his knees and raised his arms to the heavens in a very over-dramatic way.

'Maybe people would like you better if you didn't chew toilet brushes and possibly considered brushing your teeth?' said Jake, who was very quickly running out of patience, because they only had one night to track down the Glub and they hadn't even managed to get out of the back garden yet. Ajay, who had no idea about the toilet brush chewing, looked horrified at the very thought.

'I do brush my teeth!' snapped Keith the bog troll, standing up and folding his arms over his chest in a very indignant manner. 'Why I brushed them earlier today! In your bathroom, just after I'd drunk the toilet water…but before I chewed the toilet brush – 'cause I hadn't spotted that yet.'

'Exactly *where* did you get a toothbrush from?' asked Jake in a very stern voice.

Keith the bog troll thought for a very long moment, 'Eeerrrm, let me think…. Oh yes, I remember, I borrowed one from the pot on the windowsill,' he beamed.

'WHICH.   BRUSH.   DID.   YOU. '*BORROW*'????'

Jake's face had turned bright red and he looked like he was about to explode.

Keith adopted a thoughtful expression and tapped a bony digit against his chin and made '*hmmm*' noises. 'Ah yes, I remember,' he announced finally, 'it was the green one, with the nice soft bristles.'

Jake let out a sigh of relief, 'Okay, that's Lucy's brush, that's fine.'

Ajay chuckled at the thought of Lucy brushing her teeth with the same brush as the stinky bog troll. 'That's actually pretty funny and also totally gross,' he said. 'But right now, we need to figure out how we're going to get into 'The Ship.''

Jake touched the top of his head again; a good idea was coming through. 'I've got it!' He snapped his fingers, 'Wait here a minute, I've got a plan to sneak us in — I've just got to get some stuff from the house.' And with that, he ran back inside.

'You might want to bring the books along,' Keith called after him. 'That way, if we catch them, we can suck them straight back into the books.' Jake turned and gave him two thumbs up, 'Good idea, I'll bring those too.'

Walking through Bisby at night was an *interesting* experience — especially while wearing giant raincoats with big floppy hats, carrying giant fishing nets and wearing a pair of Jake's mum's high heels wedged into a pair of wellies, in a not-very-good attempt to look tall enough to get into The Ship! It wasn't so much walking as it was wobbling.

'This is literally the worst disguise anyone has ever worn in the whole entire history of disguises,' moaned Ajay, who was trying very hard not to face-plant into the footpath. Keith's big bog troll feet were far too big for the high heels, but he had managed to squish them into a pair of dad's old wellies. Luckily, he was already a bit taller than the boys, so he was slightly more able to pass for a grown-up. — A very short grown up with pointy ears and very stinky breath.

Anyone seeing the three of them wobbling down the dimly lit lane would have thought them a very strange sight indeed. Even in Bisby by the Sea you don't often find people walking around dressed as not-very-convincing fishermen in the middle of the night. But luck was on the boys' side and they went undetected. At one point a young lady on a bike passed them by, but she seemed to have something important on her mind and she paid them no attention.

Before long, the warm lights of 'The Ship Inn'

came into view up ahead. The building was hundreds of years old — and it showed. The walls sort of sagged a bit and the windows were thick and criss-crossed with lead. When you peered through them, everything looked wobbly, like the windows were melting (or you'd drunk too many bottles of fizzy pop.) The roof was beautifully thatched, and lit up with multi-coloured fairy lights. When you stepped inside, the doorways were really small, and the floors were always sticky, and the low ceiling was held up by thick wooden beams which were just at the right height for grown ups to bang their head on.

Jake and Ajay and Keith the bog troll all tucked themselves into a shadowy hedgerow and stared out at the pub. From their hiding place, everything looked normal. The sound of music and laughter drifted on the breeze and no-one was panicking or screaming the way one might if one's quiet evening had suddenly been interrupted by the arrival of a small potatoey looking creature riding a miniature rhino. Everything looked entirely normal. Until that is, Jake spotted something moving around up on the thatched roof. A strange shape was silhouetted in the moonlight. He blinked a few times to be sure he wasn't seeing things, then he pinched himself to make sure he wasn't dreaming the whole thing, but he definitely wasn't. 'There,' he whispered, 'up on the roof!'

And there they were! The nefarious Glub and the book-rhino had somehow managed to find their way up onto the roof of The Ship, and the pair of them were bouncing around up there like a pair of seagulls on space-hoppers. Luckily, no-one below had spotted them yet, and it looked as though the Glub hadn't spotted the boys and Keith the bog troll either. 'Okay,' whispered Ajay, hefting the satchel of books on to his shoulder. 'What do we do now?'

'I could *whoosh* up the drainpipe to the roof,' suggested Keith. 'I can try and suck them back into the books before anyone sees them and then its.... Oops! Too late!'

The boys watched in horror as the Glub and the book-rhino flew up in the air in a particularly large bounce, but instead of landing back on the roof, they fell straight down the chimney and into the pub!

'Oooh, that's torn it!' gasped Keith. 'They'd better hope Santa doesn't find out! Going down the chimney's sort of his special thing and he gets *very* cranky when people try to rip him off!'

'Come on!' Jake had already started wobble-running towards the pub. Ajay and Keith the bog troll tottered after him with their floppy hats and fishing nets flailing around wildly as they tried to catch up.

The scene that met them when they sneaked through the door was one of total, utter chaos! A rock band was playing on the stage and everyone was having a fantastic time throwing themselves around and bouncing up and down in time to the music. No one even noticed the three *very* unusual looking and quite short fishermen creeping in through the door.

'OH NO!!!' wailed Keith. 'It's the Beatles all over again... *Look*!' He stretched out one of his knobbly fingers and pointed towards the stage. At first Jake and Ajay couldn't see what he was pointing at, everything looked just fine. The singer was singing and pointing at the crowd and whirling around with his microphone stand. The guitarist was strumming away with his legs spread wide, like a true guitar hero should. The bass player was grooving along while looking really cool and disinterested and the drummer was bashing away at…Oh! Oh no!

The Nefarious Glub

The Glub had managed to find its way onto the drumkit and was merrily hopping around from drum to drum, while the poor confused drummer tried to *bop* it with his sticks! Jake could see the drummer furiously yelling, '*Oi! Get off!*' at the curious little creature as he tried to bash it with his drumsticks and keep the beat going at the same time.

'I can see the Glub,' shouted Ajay over the noise of the band, 'but where's the rhino?'

'No idea!' bellowed Keith, shrugging his bony shoulders. Jake, who was standing with his fingers in his ears, was starting to look very stressed indeed. He hated loud noises, and the band were getting a little bit louder every time the drummer tried to *whack* the Glub.

Ajay pleaded with Keith, 'We have to move fast,

Jake can't stand the noise in here and the Glub won't stay on the drums for much longer, what do we do?'

'Don't panic buddy, I've got this!' A peculiar expression crept across Keith's face and he pulled himself up to his full-not-very-tall height and puffed out his chest.

'You're not going to do anything *silly* are you?' shouted Ajay over the music. He really was starting to feel most suspicious about what Keith had planned.

'Silly? Me? Naah! Don't stress it dude, I'll be careful. — I'll be subtle like a Ninja, or a peacock or a polar bear or whatever!'

Before Ajay could point out that neither peacocks nor polar bears are famous for their subtlety, Keith had leapt up onto the nearest table, thrown off his giant raincoat disguise and exposed his full raggedy bog-trollness to the whole crowd. Then, he curled his thin lips back revealing a mouthful of rotten yellow teeth with bits of old loo roll stuck between them.

'No!' pleaded Ajay. 'Don't!'

But it was too late.

Keith the bog troll stuck two fingers in his mouth and unleashed the single LOUDEST, most earpiercing *whistle* that the world has ever heard! LOUDER than the band! LOUDER than ten bands! LOUDER than a hundred jumbo jets! LOUDER than a thousand pneumatic drills. EVEN LOUDER than an angry mum when it's the fifth time she's called you downstairs for dinner and she's started to get **REALLY** cross! It was so loud that every dog for a hundred miles stopped sniffing other dog's bottoms and looked in the direction of Bisby. And everyone in 'The Ship' stopped talking or dancing or playing or singing and stared in horrified silence at the hideous bog troll creature who was standing on a table as though a troll on a table was a perfectly normal thing.

(Everyone except Jake, who was still standing with his eyes scrunched tightly shut and his fingers wedged firmly in his ears.)

'Attention everyone! Attention please,' Keith clapped his hands together like a teacher does when they want the class to be quiet. 'My name is Keith and I'm a bog troll. Its lovely to meet you all and I'm sorry to interrupt your lovely evening. But I have some important news! I hate to be the one to tell you this, but...' — He took a deep, deep breath, pointed at the drumkit and, at the top of his voice, screamed,

'THERE'S A GLUB! A GLUB! A GLUB IS IN THE PUB!'

The nefarious Glub saw its moment and leapt up from the drum-kit. It stuck out its gross purple tongue and let out the longest, nastiest, smelliest, most disgusting fart anyone has ever heard — *PAAAAAAAARRRRRP!*

'EEEEEWWWWWW!'

Shouted the poor drummer, who caught the full blast right in his face!

'EEEEERRRRGGHH!'

Yelled the bass player, who was also standing in the blast zone!

'AAAAARRRGGGH! A TROLL!'

Screamed everybody else.

. . .

'THERE'S A TROLL ON THE TABLE! ABANDON SHIP! RUN!'

Keith's jaw dropped open, 'Wait, hang on, what did *I* do?' He was completely taken aback that people were more scared of him — a lanky green bog troll with disgusting yellow teeth — than they were of a small, angry, flatulent potato-poo creature. 'No!' he cried. 'Not me, I'm not the scary one! It's the Glub! The *Glub*! It's nefarious! It's a nefarious Glub!'

But it was too late — the stampede had already begun.

People were shoving and pushing and clamouring to get out through the Ship's tiny door. On the stage, the poor drummer had fainted face down into his drumkit from the smell. The guitarist had hidden behind his giant speakers and the singer was long gone. The bass player was still there, fiddling with her bass guitar and muttering something about 'new strings'.

At that moment, the book-rhino finally showed up! It had apparently got its pointy little horn stuck on the way down the chimney and it had taken the vibrations from the Glub's disgusting bottom-burp to coax it free. The tiny rhino came crashing down into the fireplace where it landed with a resounding **THUD!** The bewildered beast slid across the floor on its bottom until it came to a halt in a pile of thick, black soot.

In less than a minute, The Ship had gone from being packed full of people enjoying themselves, to being completely deserted and covered in soot. The only people left were Ajay — who was clutching his head in his hands, Keith the bog troll — who was still standing on the table looking utterly bemused, and Jake — who still had his eyes tight shut and his fingers in his ears.

...And the runaway book creatures.

The Glub gave an evil cackle, hopped onto the sooty book-rhino and sang out, 'Nah nah nah naaah naaah! Can't catch me *suckers*!' Then the evil little monster stuck out its tongue once more and, with a quick *pffft* from its toxic bottom, the gruesome twosome shot out the door and darted off into the night once more.

'Well that went well,' said Keith, hopping down from the table. 'Great band, I thought they had a really funky groove, didn't you?'

'What did I miss?' asked Jake, finally pulling his fingers out of his ears and opening his eyes.

Ajay sighed, 'They got away.'

8

Glunting

'SO, TELL ME,' said Jake as they plodded towards the centre of Bisby, leaving the carnage of The Ship behind them. — 'What exactly *is* a nefarious Glub? I mean, what's the big deal? It's pretty small, so it can't exactly be that dangerous can it?' Ajay, who was picking soot out of his nose, nodded in agreement. He had been wondering the same thing ever since Jake and Keith the bog troll had dragged him into this whole crazy adventure.

'What's a Glub!' Keith raged. 'What's a Glub? WHAT'S A GLUB!? — How can you not know what a Glub is? We've just chased one out of a pub!'

'No, I don't mean it like that, I mean, what does it do? Where does it come from? And why is it being such a pain in the butt?'

'Oh!' Keith, thought for moment, pulled a large chunk of hairy, yellow wax out of his left ear, stared at it, and then popped it into his mouth. 'Well,' he said, chewing away on his revolting snack, 'They come from a book.'

Jake looked cross, 'I know that silly, so did you, but how and why?'

'Well,' said Keith, gulping down the chunk of earwax. 'Whenever a writer imagines something, be it a new kind of creature, or a fantastical faraway land. That idea becomes real in that writer's mind. And then, when they put that idea into a book, it becomes real in the mind of anyone that reads that book. It's called imagination. And imagination is basically just a different kind of magic, a bit like how a magician pulls a rabbit out of a hat, or a coin from behind an ear. And if something goes *in* by magic, then it can come *out* by magic.'

To illustrate his point, Keith reached behind Ajay's ear and produced a shiny gold coin. 'That's not magic!' said Jake, who was starting to feel as though he had just about had enough of the bog troll. 'That's just a silly trick, I know because I had a magician set for Christmas, and the instructions showed me how to do it.'

Keith the bog troll gave Jake a long hard stare, 'My dear Sir, it most certainly *is* magic!'

'Is not.'

'IS SO!'

'IS NOT!'

'IS! IS! IS! IS! — Did your magic set show you how to do this?' Keith reached behind Jake's ear, which was a terrible idea, because Jake hated being touched by people he didn't know, especially if they were smelly bog trolls!

'STOP IT! WHY CAN'T YOU JUST GO AWAY AND LEAVE ME ALONE!'

Jake screamed in Keith's face and sat down on the pavement with angry tears streaming down his cheeks.

Poor Keith was stunned. He hadn't meant to upset Jake; he had only wanted to pull an actual real-life toilet roll with a rabbit in out from behind his ear. It was his best trick. No-one had ever screamed at him *before* he'd pulled a toilet roll with a rabbit in out from behind their ear before. (It sometimes happened afterwards though.)

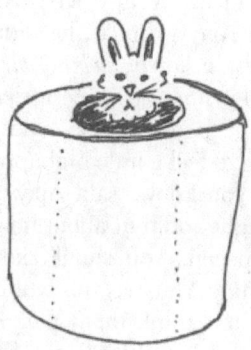

'I'm sorry, please don't cry,' he sat down cross-legged on the floor next to Jake. 'I know this isn't how you expected to spend your sleep over, chasing around town in the middle of the night and getting all covered in soot.'

Jake pulled his knees up close to his face and tried to make himself as small as possible, 'I'm not like you,' he sniffed between sobs. 'I'm not a magic creature who *whooshes* around in pipes and has adventures. I like things to stay the way I like them. I like watching my films, and I like reading my graphic novels about *other people* having adventures.' A big bogey bubble popped out of his nose and he sniffed it away. 'But I *don't* like having them myself. Its late and I'm tired and I never wanted those stupid books in the first place. I hate magical creatures and I want to go home.'

Keith the bog troll gave a big sigh, 'Oh Jake, we're all magical creatures in our own way! It's what makes your world such an interesting place to visit. — Can you imagine how boring it would be if everyone was the same? I mean look at my new friend Ajay here, he's *hideous*! But once you get past how incredibly, insanely, *unbelievably* ugly he is, he's actually quite nice!' A tiny smile flickered across Jake's face and Ajay grinned, he didn't mind being called incredibly, insanely, *unbelievably* ugly by a revolting bog troll if it made his best friend feel better.

'I suppose he is quite nice,' said Jake, who was actually starting to feel a little bit happier.

'He's right you know,' said Ajay. 'Not about me being ugly I might add, but about how we're all a bit magical and special. You should know that better than anyone Jake. You see the world differently to most people, but I think that's part of what makes you such brilliant fun to be around. Sometimes a different point of view helps to figure things out!'

Jake rubbed away his tears and nodded so vigorously that his hair flew up and down like a wig from a joke shop. All his life people had told him he was different because of the way his brain was wired up. Sometimes they were nice and sometimes they weren't, and sometimes it made things really tricky, but never when Ajay was around. He was even able to make hanging around with a bog troll in the middle of the night seem safe and familiar. 'Thank you,' Jake said finally, while doing an outside-his-head smile, so they knew he really meant it. 'So, tell me about the Glub then. What exactly is he?'

'The nefarious Glub is a very unique magical creature,' replied Keith, rummaging around for another chunk of ear wax to munch on. 'Just like me, he started out as somebody's idea, brought to life in a book. The problem is that hardly anybody ever read the Glub's book. It's spent nearly all of its life squished up on a shelf or forgotten in a dusty pile at the back of the library cupboard. For years and years now, the Glub has stayed put in his book, getting more and more fed up and more and more nefarious. That is until Mrs Crisp came along and emptied out the cupboard.'

'I knew it!' Jake leapt to his feet, suddenly feeling a lot better. 'She's a witch or a wizard or something. She made me look into this weird, spinning thing and before I knew what was happening, I ended up with a pile of stinky old books and a troll in my downstairs toilet.'

Keith looked very put out at that, 'How very dare you!' he gasped. 'My book is NOT stinky!' Jake and Ajay both gave him a long hard stare. 'Okay,' he admitted, 'well, it's not as stinky as the Glub's book anyway. But that's beside the point! The point is that the Glub hasn't existed in anyone's imagination for such a long time, that he's become a gross, twisted, angry little monster! A grumpy little beast who desperately craves attention and will do anything to get it, no matter how…well…*nefarious*! That's why every time he gets out of his book, he goes looking for people to show off to. And when he doesn't get attention, things start to get ugly.'

'How so?' asked Ajay.

'Well, that's when he does *extra*-nefarious things, usually something really naughty, like breaking stuff. *Big* stuff.'

'Oh dear,' said Jake. 'That doesn't sound good. But what about Mrs Crisp and her weird spin-o-scope or whatever it's called, what does *she* have to do with anything?'

'The 'praxinoscope,' said Keith. 'Every magical book creature knows about it, but none of us knows how it works. All I can tell you about that, is that it's a very old way of telling stories, and that stories are magical things. Why, we're making our own story right now! One day you might choose to write all of this down in a book of your own. And then this most strange and wonderful night will happen over and over in the minds of children everywhere. You see, magic has a special energy all of its own Jake, and I should imagine that when you have lots of something as magical as stories all together in one place — like a library — anything could happen. Magic is a very strange and marvellous thing Jake. I wish I had all the answers for you, really, I do, but I don't. After all, I'm only a bog troll, and not a very smart one at that. I think that maybe you should speak to Mrs Crisp about it when you return the books.'

'You're not *only* a bog troll, you're our friend, Keith the bog troll, and I think you're very smart,' said Ajay giving him a friendly nudge in the ribs. 'After all, you figured out where the Glub would go. But Jake's right — if we don't find the Glub and his little rhino friend soon, and get them back in the books, then who-knows-what might happen. So, let's get Glub-hunting!'

'Glunting! laughed Keith, we're Glunters!

'I like that chuckled Ajay, we're the 'Glunter gang!'

'Yes, very good. But where exactly should we be 'glunting?' said Jake — who was always very practical.

'Actually, I think I might have an idea about that,' said Ajay. 'Think about it, if you were new in town, what's the biggest, brightest most obvious place to head towards?'

Keith shrugged his shoulders, 'Don't ask me, I live in a book!'

Jake didn't say anything, he had already started running down the hill, 'Come on!' he yelled over his shoulder.

9

Aaaand its Gone

THE FERRIS WHEEL came to Bisby sea front every other summer. It was a marvellous looking thing; most Ferris wheels nowadays are painted bright white and look very modern and hi-tech. But not the Bisby wheel. The one that came to Bisby by the Sea was a fantastic old beast. It was painted in a deep maroon colour and decorated with swirls and patterns and hundreds of tiny lights all the way around it. Its old-fashioned wooden construction creaked and squeaked as it went around and around, and crackly old organ music blared out of hidden speakers, whisking the riders away on a journey into times gone by. Jake had ridden it lots of times over the years, always hanging on tightly to his mum and dad, because being that high made him nervous and feel a bit sick. But it was worth it for the view out over the town and over to the Isle of Clod.

Jake and Ajay and Keith the bog troll stared up at the gigantic wheel towering above them. The sea wind had picked up and it whipped through its beams, making the old wheel groan and creak like an elderly giant. The little carriages that you sat in rocked back and forth, and the tarpaulin covering the pay booth flapped and banged against the time-worn paint. 'This actually seems like a pretty good place to start looking,' said Keith. 'I reckon you might be onto something here. If the Glub's going to head towards anything, it's bound to be this!'

As he spoke, the Bisby church clock started to chime,

Bong!
Bong! Bong!

Keith and Ajay cocked their heads against the wind and listened,

Bong! Bong!
Bong! Bong!

But between the *howling* wind and the *flapping* tarpaulin and the *groaning* and *creaking* wheel and the *swish* of the waves and the *bonging* of the church clock, the unlikely gang of glunters had missed one very important sound… The sound of book-rhino hooves *pattering* their way along the deserted sea front as the nefarious Glub sneaked up behind them.

Bong!

Went the church clock.

Bong! Bong!
Bong! Bong!

'Midnight,' said Ajay grimly, 'and no sign of the Glub.'

'The witching hour,' whispered Keith in his most mysterious voice, 'when magic is at its most powerful.'

'Do you think he'll show up soon?' asked Jake, who was reading the time off his walkie watch instead of listening to the clock.

'HE WHO SMELT IT DEALT IT!' shrieked the sneaky Glub, before bending over and unleashing a mighty blast of bum-gas right behind Keith and the

boys! A blast of nothing less than gargantuan proportions!

The blast to end all blasts!

Ppppppaaaarrrrrpppp!

'Oh no! Oh help, I can't breathe! Oh, that's awful — and I spend most of my time in other people's toilets!' gasped Keith, dropping to the floor and shoving a bony finger up each of his nostrils right up to the knuckle.

Jake and Ajay were powerless to help him, each of them had also fallen foul of the Glub's despicable sneak attack. Jake's eyes were streaming with tears as the pernicious odour surrounded him, '*Gack!* He coughed, *hurgh!* Oh, my stars, it's…*bluurgh!*'

Ajay, who was also engulfed by the noxious fumes, flailed his arms around in a desperate attempt to fight his way free from the overwhelming cloud of stench. '*Glurrrp*,' he choked, cupping a hand in front of his mouth, trying to stop himself from blowing regurgitated chunks of his tea all over the floor.

The Glub seized the advantage that his toxic bottom had provided and hopped up onto the bookrhino's back. The pair of them bounced across the three stricken glunters using their heads as steppingstones.

Bounce! 'OW!'
Bounce! 'OW!'
Bounce! 'OW!'

Using Jake's head as a trampoline, the nefarious Glub leapt high into the air and performed another of its really quite impressive loop-the-loops. The nasty little beast landed in one of the carriages on the Ferris wheel and sneered down at the three friends still rolling around on the floor below. 'And now I'd say it's time to go, so hit the button friend rhino!' it sang.

Jake and Ajay and Keith the bog troll stared in disbelief as the book-rhino used its horn to barge open the door to the little control room for the Ferris wheel. It stomped one of its hooved feet down on the 'start' button and used its horn to nudge the speed control slider — the mighty wheel creaked once and then slowly began to turn around. The rhino nudged the slider again, this time it went past the **FAST** setting and the wheel really sprang to life, spinning around and around, quickly gaining speed. Then the slider went past the **REALLY, REALLY FAST** setting, and the wheel span even faster still. Finally, the rhino nudged the slider past the **ARE YOU INSANE?** setting, and the wheel stopped looking like a wheel at all, and instead became just a big whizzy blur.

'STOP!' called Keith. 'Please rhino, you have to stop!' But the book-rhino didn't listen. Keith and the boys couldn't even see the Glub anymore, the wheel was spinning so fast that it was impossible to see anything other than a giant maroon smudge whirling around in a cacophony of *clanking* and *banging*.

'It's going to blow!' yelled Keith. 'LOOK OUT!'

First came a sort of *hiss*! like a big angry snake.

Then there was a gigantic **CRACK!** that tore through the night sky.

But the next sound was the scariest of all. A *creaking*, *wailing*, *moaning* sound filled the air. A mournful **shriek** that sounded as if the very soul of the wonderful old Ferris wheel was pleading for mercy. It was a sound *so* loud and *so* terrible that you didn't just hear it with your ears, but you felt it deep inside your chest, you tasted it with your tongue, and it made your eyeballs wobble in their sockets and your spine shiver.

Then, with one last tremendous

Screeeeecchh!

the old Ferris wheel blew clear of its mountings and flew off down Bisby sea front like a giant hamster ball. Only it wasn't a hamster riding the catastrophe-waiting-to-happen. It was a Glub. A most nefarious Glub!

As the wheel shot past, the rhino stuck its horn into one of the carriages and flew up in the air to join its partner in crime, and off they went together — a pair of disgruntled magical creatures riding a runaway vintage Ferris wheel at great speed through Bisby by the Sea. Leaving Jake and Ajay and Keith the bog troll staring after them in a cloud of stinking Glub gas!

10

Oh, It's Coming Back!

'WELL,' said Keith. 'I'll be honest, I did *not* see that coming!'

'I think we *may* have just lost the element of surprise,' said Ajay, rubbing the top of his head where the Glub had bounced on it.

'My mum is going to kill me,' said Jake. 'Stealing her heels, ruining a gig and emptying a pub was one thing. But *this*! This is a *whole* new level of 'in trouble'! The whole town is going to see this!'

Every part of him wanted to curl up in a ball and scream until the world went away. But somehow, he didn't…Because the more he thought about the rogue Ferris wheel tearing off towards the centre of Bisby, the more he realised that he knew precisely what was about to happen.

Dear reader, do you remember that right back at the very start of this story, I explained to you that Jake sees the world a little differently to most people? Well, as it happens, seeing the world a little differently can come in very, *very* handy sometimes. In fact, every now and then, it can save the day. — Because you see, this situation was *exactly* the sort of thing that Jake *did* often wonder about. The kind of thing that nobody else but him ever seemed to wonder about at all!

Like the time he had seen a bus trip full of old ladies with bright purple hair arrive in Bisby. Instead of parking at the big car park up near the chine, the driver had tried to save the ladies from having to walk down the hill, so he had brought the bus right down into Bisby. But, of course, the streets were *far* too narrow, and the houses were *far* too close together, and of course, the bus had got stuck.

It had taken the driver a very long time and a lot of shouting to get the bus out. And, as he had sat there in the Dubster watching the whole saga unfold, Jake had wondered what would happen if they just couldn't ever get it out. — Would the bus just have to stay there forever, wedged across Bisby high street? Or would they make a hole in the middle of it for cars to drive through? Or would someone have to come along and chop it up and take it out piece by piece? But then how would they get the pieces out if the high street was too small for a crane? When he had asked mum about it, she had just done a *tutsigh*, and told him it wasn't worth worrying about. But how did she know that? What if it happened again?

Why am I telling you this dear reader?
Simple. As I have already mentioned, Jake had

visited the Ferris wheel many times in the past, and each of those times he had stood patiently in the queue, waiting his turn and staring up at the marvellous machine. And each time, as he stared up at the Ferris wheel, he would find himself wondering what would happen were it to break free of its moorings and trundle off down the road. He had asked both his mum and his dad what they thought would happen, but neither of them had given it much thought. Instead, they assumed he was afraid and tried to insist that it wasn't worth thinking about because such a thing could never happen.

But Jake *had* given it some thought. He had given it *plenty* of thought! Because, just like the stuck bus, Jake could see no reason why it *shouldn't* happen. So, when his turn had come to go up on the wheel, he had always made sure to look out for where it would end up if it ever *were* to come loose. And, although he certainly hadn't expected it to be as a result of a magical malicious potato/poo creature (Poo-tato?) and a misguided miniature rhino, nonetheless, the result was the same. The wheel *had* come loose and was, at that very moment, thundering its way along Bisby seafront towards 'The Fancy Pasty'. Where, in a few moments, it would reach the point where the hill got really steep and the Dubster always started to struggle. Which meant that in a few *more* moments, it would run out of steam and come crashing straight back down the hill towards them! And at quite some speed!

'Quick!' shouted Keith. 'After it!'

He started to dash off after the errant wheel, but Jake called out to him, 'No! Stop, wait!' Keith and Ajay both stared at Jake as though he had gone completely potty. 'It won't make it up the hill,' he explained. 'Trust me, it's too steep. It'll be coming back this way any minute and if we don't find a way to

Oh, It's Coming Back!

stop it...' He waved a thumb over his shoulder towards the pier.

The Bisby pier dated back to Victorian times and unlike many modern piers, it didn't have a fancy arcade at the end with a go-Kart track and rides that made your insides go squishy. Instead, Bisby pier was home to a selection of antique slot machines, a 'Punch and Judy' show, a few stalls selling 'Kiss me Quick' hats, candyfloss, and lollies shaped like dummies — and a large bouncy castle that you weren't allowed to use on a windy day. The high-speed runaway Ferris wheel was easily heavy enough to smash straight through the whole lot without stopping and was doomed to end up at the bottom of Bisby Bay, taking the Glub and the book-rhino along with it.

'Oh no!' cried Keith. 'He's right! The pier will be smashed to pieces, and so will the Glub and the rhino! They'll be bashed to bits and dunked to death in Bisby bay. What do we do? It's a disaster!

'We have to stop it before it comes back,' said Ajay. 'But how?' The glunter gang stared at each other hopelessly, how could two small boys and one smelly bog troll hope to stop a giant runaway Ferris wheel?

While the Glub hunters were considering their impending fate, the Glub himself was having a whale of a time! He and the rhino had wedged themselves into one of the carriages and they had both stuck their heads out the side of the careening wheel as it flew up the high street, like when a dog sticks it's head out of a car window.

'WEEEEEEE!' squealed the nefarious Glub as the wheel bounced over the cobbles, knocking over dustbins and signposts as it went.

'.................!' said the

rhino, who didn't say much, because rhinos don't speak — even miniature magical book-rhinos — but he looked like he was having a great time.

THUMP! The sign for the beach went flying.

WHACK! That was the novelty dustbin outside the rock shop, the wheel squashed it flat as a pancake.

WALLOP! That was the cheerful 'Chip man' statue outside the chippy, he didn't look so happy without a head! Hotdog man was next to fall, swiftly followed by the oversized plastic ice-cream and the giant donut with sprinkles that Jake liked to poke his head through every time he passed by it. One by one, the giant wheel flattened all the fun and exciting bits of Bisby high street. The nefarious Glub looked thrilled to be causing so much carnage! But what the little creep had failed to notice, was that all the time, the hill was getting steeper and steeper…and the wheel was starting to spin slower and slower!

Back at the bottom of the hill, down by the pier, Jake and the others were getting desperate. They could hear the smashing and crashing as the wheel made its way up the high street and they knew that time was running out. 'What about a really, really big net?' said Keith. 'We could catch it in a big net.'

'Brilliant!' cheered Ajay. 'The only flaw in your otherwise perfect plan is the fact that WE DON'T HAVE A REALLY, REALLY BIG NET!'

'Oh yeah, right,' grumbled Keith. 'I suppose we don't. Well what *do* we have?'

Each of them looked around for inspiration, but there was nothing nearby that stood any chance at all of catching the Ferris wheel.

'The bouncy castle might slow it down a bit,' suggested Jake, looking up at the bright yellow structure. It was painted to look like a mediaeval castle, right down to the giant pictures of a gallant knight and a fair maiden.

'Actually, it might,' replied Ajay. 'But it probably won't be enough on its own. If we had something else — something to slow the wheel down a bit before it got to the bouncy castle, that might just work. Any ideas Keith?'

Keith didn't reply, he was staring intently at a nearby manhole cover and doing what looked like mental maths calculations on his fingers. His lips were moving very fast as he counted, and every so often he would turn and squint up the hill in the direction of the town centre. Eventually, he nodded to himself and turned to the boys, 'I've got it!' he announced, sounding unusually serious. 'I reckon we've got about two minutes at the most before that wheel comes smashing back through here, takes out the pier and dumps whatever's left of the Glub and the rhino in the drink. They might be pains in the butt, but I don't want them to end up like that. I've done some thinking, and I reckon that if Santa can visit almost every single child in the world in one night, then I can hop down that manhole and *whoosh* my way to every bathroom in Bisby in under two minutes — if I *whoosh* really fast. As in *really* fast — faster than I've ever *whooshed* before. Probably faster than *any* bog-troll has ever *whooshed* before.'

'Why?' asked Jake. 'What's the point in that?'

'Ah ha!' replied Keith, tapping a bony digit against the side of his nose and winking. 'Can you imagine how many towels and flannels and sponges and laundry baskets there are in every bathroom in Bisby?'

Ajay's jaw dropped, 'He's right! There must be hundreds, thousands even!'

'Right, and all those laundry baskets will be packed with smelly clothes, maybe even enough to stop a runaway Ferris wheel!' said Keith with a grin.

'I dunno,' said Jake, looking dubious. 'That's a lot of skiddy pants and manky towels to stack up.'

'Then let's get stacking!' cried Keith. With a brisk salute, he yanked up the manhole cover and *whooshed* off into the fetid, stinky sewers beneath.

11

The Pantsicade

JAKE WAS JUST ABOUT to apologise to Ajay for dragging him into such a mess, when a plume of pants and knickers and bras and soggy towels came flying out of the manhole. 'Blimey! gasped Ajay. 'That was qui…' but before he could finish speaking, a sweaty t-shirt flew out of the hole and landed on his head.

'Come on, we need to get stacking,' called out Jake, frantically scrabbling around and forming a pile of clothes. What had started out as a few bits of underwear flying through the air had very quickly turned into a full-blown laundry fountain, it was as though somebody had turned on a hosepipe (clothespipe!) and was spraying the boys with it on full blast!

Deep in the sewer pipes of Bisby, Keith was *whooshing* around faster than he had ever dreamed possible. With each passing second, he would *whizz* round another U-bend and pop out of another toilet bowl. Once in the empty bathroom he would grab anything soft he could lay his hands on, *whoosh* back to the manhole and hurl it high into the air before heading off again. Occasionally, a toilet would be occupied, and he would have to *screech* to a halt at the last second to avoid bashing someone on the bottom!

All over Bisby, people were being woken from their slumber by strange sounds coming from their plumbing. But few would have imagined that the ruckus was being caused by a magical bog troll hurtling around in the pipes behind their walls and under their floors while clutching handfuls of borrowed laundry.

Back on the seafront, the ghastly plume of dirty clothes exploding out of the manhole had grown to monumental proportions. The filthy fountain reached up at least thirty metres into the air, showering Jake and Ajay with all manner of stinky clothes and squelchy towels, which the boys piled together to form the world's smelliest, soggiest barricade. There were socks with holes in and vests with curry down the front, towels still dripping from bedtime baths and novelty sponges shaped like penguins. There were pullovers, cardigans, big pants, small pants, frilly pants and stinky pants, fancy dresses, wedding dresses, blouses and trousers, boots and suits. — Anything at all that you could ever imagine that might be found in a bathroom came flying up out the hole and plopped down atop the ever-expanding barricade.

Bibs fell on wigs; skirts fell on shirts and hats fell on bathmats. It was a clothing cascade! A washing waterfall! A smelly tsunami! A geyser of grossness! All forming a monumental barricade – a pantsicade!

Eventually, the pile had grown so big that Jake and Ajay got a bit scared of getting stuck at the top, so they gave up trying to stack the clothes, and instead started to climb back down the mountainous heap of stinky washing as fast as they could. 'We don't have long!' shouted Jake, who was trying to untangle himself from a pair of skinny jeans with rips in. 'Do you think it's big enough?'

Ajay, who was struggling with a particularly big pair of pants, yelled back, 'I don't know, I've never tried to catch a runaway Ferris wheel with a massive pile of other people's dirty washing before!'

'Fair point!' replied Jake, who had managed to find a shiny sleeping bag and was preparing to ride it down the massive stinking heap like a toboggan.

Meanwhile, at the top of the hill, the Ferris wheel had finally slowed to a halt. It tottered for an instant and teetered for a moment. Not going forwards, but not quite ready to tumble backwards either. The Glub and the rhino — neither of which were terribly bright — had no clue what was about to happen to them. For their minds were full of only one thing — mischief! And a mind full of mischief has very little room left for complicated thinking about such scientific matters as *momentum*. Which is a fancy science word for what the wheel had just run out of. A very clever scientist or a teacher might explain momentum to you by grabbing some chalk or a pen and scribbling on the nearest board, and this is what they would write:

$$P = MV$$

Which is a very fancy scientific way of saying momentum = mass x velocity.

Now then reader, neither you nor I need to understand such complicated mathematical matters right now. But what I *can* tell you, is that P = MV was very bad news for the nefarious Glub and its unwitting rhino companion. Very bad news indeed. Because it meant that they were about to go backwards, very, very, *very* quickly!

The Glub first realised something was wrong when he saw the bemused book-rhino float past him like an astronaut's lost pen might float about in a spaceship. The nasty little beast barely had time to let out a squeaky little scared-fart, before gravity finally got the better of the runaway Ferris wheel, and the Glub and the rhino began their descent back down Bisby high street towards the waiting barricade of 'borrowed' laundry.

Because of science, the wheel was much MUCH faster on the way back down! Round and round it flew, clattering and banging like thunder. Suddenly the Glub wasn't having quite so much fun anymore, with nothing left to squash or break, there was nothing to slow the thunderous descent. Shattered bits of plastic donut and hotdog man flew out behind the battered old Ferris wheel like the wake of a speedboat. Up above, curtains twitched, and eyeballs bulged as the good people of Bisby, woken by the calamitous racket, watched in horror as the Ferris wheel tore down their beloved high street. But inside the wrecked remains of the carriage, the Glub was about to meet his just desserts…and his just breakfast…and his just lunch! Up and down he flew, up and down and round and round, *bouncing* and *bonking* and *boinking* and *bumping* into the floor, then the ceiling, then the rhino, then the floor again, then the ceiling again, then the rhino again. Until his little Glubby tummy could take no more! In one mighty heave, the nefarious Glub emptied the contents of his stomach all over the inside of the tumbling carriage.

'Hhhhwwwoooaaaarrrrgggghhh!'

It was like being inside a washing machine full of his own vomit! The rhino took one whiff of the second-hand carrot plastering the place and immediately added his own technicolour explosion to the proceedings!

'Bllleeeeuuuuuuurrrrrgggghhh!'

Dearest reader, it is my most solemn duty to inform you, that to this very day, there has never been placed on record an incident where more chunks were blown, than that fateful night in the runaway Ferris wheel.

If '*most amount of puke ever*

to be puked' was a category in the world record book, you would surely find a picture of the Glub and the rhino on that very page, looking as they did that night, completely covered from horn to hoof in gross, glistening chunks of vomitious vomit! Eurgh!

At the bottom of the hill, Jake and Ajay braced themselves for what was to come. Keith the bog troll popped up out of the manhole with a toothbrush sticking out of each nostril. 'Wow!' he gasped yanking them out and staggering towards the enormous pile the boys had created, 'That's a lot of dirty pants!' Then, with an exhausted sigh, his eyes rolled back in his head and poor Keith collapsed in a heap.

Jake yelled at Ajay, 'Quick, grab his other arm, we've got to get him out of the way, or he'll be squashed like a bug-troll!' The two boys dashed over to help their fallen friend, but just as they took him by the wrists, a thunderous sound filled the air.

It wasn't a sound you heard every day; it certainly wasn't a sound I can truly recreate for you here on this page! — It was the sound of a vintage Ferris wheel filled with mischievous magical creatures and sloshing sick hurtling down the hill towards the boys like a monstrous vomit comet.

It started as a deep **RRUUUUMBLE**.

Then it grew into more of a steady **ROAR**.

Pretty soon it was a barrage of **SMASHING** glass.

SPLINTERING
wood.
SNAPPING
Plastic, and...
SCRAPING metal.

An orchestral masterpiece, a symphony of destruction with the Glub as its conductor. A concerto of catastrophe that was building to its grand finale... with the boys and Keith stuck firmly in its path.

'Come on Keith,' grunted Jake. 'Please wake up!' but it was no use, Keith was completely *whooshed* out.

'He doesn't look this heavy!' panted Ajay, tugging for all his might. 'It's no use, we can't move him.'

'No,' cried Jake, 'we can't leave him here, he'll be squished.'

'You have to put me back in the book.' Keith's yellow eyes flickered open, just a little, and he wrapped his bony fingers around Jake's hand.

'KEITH!' Both boys jumped for joy, 'YOU'RE OKAY!'

'Come on Keith, we've got to move right now!' sobbed Jake.

'I'm sorry guys, but I can't move,' Keith's voice was little more than a whisper. 'I think I over did the *whooshing*, but at least I got to explore after all, this seems like a really nice town. I saw some very high-quality porcelain.'

The sound of the approaching wheel grew louder with every passing second, 'Jake, we're out of time,' said Ajay, his voice heavy with sadness.

Keith took both boys hands and held them tightly to his chest, 'This was the most awesome night *ever*,' he smiled. 'People normally just scream at bog trolls, but you guys treated me like a friend, and I'll never forget that. Thank-you, thank-you both for everything!'

'We'll always be the glunter gang,' sobbed Jake. A

large lump had formed in his throat and it was making it difficult to speak.

'You're the best bog troll I've ever met,' sniffed Ajay. 'I'm really sorry I threw a net at you! I'll never forget you, never.'

Keith's eyes glazed over for a moment and his head lolled back, just as the wheel arrived back on the seafront and began its final charge towards them. 'Do it,' he wheezed. 'Open my book, it'll magic me back in and I'll be safe and sound, back where I belong.'

Ajay hesitated, 'Will we ever see you again?'

'I don't know,' smiled Keith. 'But if you read my book then I'll always live in your imagination. — Now let's get going before we *all* get squashed!' Ajay nodded and slung the satchel from over his shoulder, he plunged in his hand and pulled out Keith's book. He handed it to Jake, 'Here, you should do it, it's your book, the magic might not work for me.'

Jake took the book and, with a deep sigh, opened it wide. Time seemed to stand still. The air shimmered like it does on a hot day, and the thundering wheel froze in place just for a second. Keith gave one last wink to his friends and swirled up into the book the way that a genie might disappear into a lamp. As he did so, the words reformed on the pages, and his image appeared once more on the front cover.

'JUMP!'

The boys dived for safety just as the Ferris wheel ploughed into the gargantuan pile of dirty washing with a somewhat underwhelming

Flump!

Pants and socks with holes in, and vests with curry on, and soggy towels and shirts and trousers and all sorts of soft things flew in every direction. It was like a tropical monsoon, but with other people's dirty laundry instead of rain. And there, right in the middle of it all, was the Ferris wheel.

'It's not stopping!' wailed Jake as the wheel tore straight through the pile.

'But it's slowing down!' yelled Ajay, pointing at the bouncy castle.

And sure enough, the battered old wheel, slowed by its collision with the whiffy washing, plopped into the bouncy castle and came to a gentle halt. The ruined ride finally wedged itself straight into the face of the fair maiden with a loud, rubbery

Creeeeaaak!

'Go! Go! Go!' bellowed Jake. 'Get the Glub!' Ajay threw himself onto the bouncy castle, which was a terrible idea, because bouncy castles are bouncy. What followed might best be described as 'a catalogue of catastrophes.' Or perhaps 'a bunch of bouncing bungles.'

The Glub, dizzied and confused by its high-speed tumble down the high street, emerged from the wrecked wheel with icky globs of sick all over it and a burning rage in its beady little eyes. Upon seeing Ajay clutching its book, the creature sensed that an unwelcome return to its pages was about to happen. And, rather than go quietly, it grabbed its trusty companion the book-rhino by the horn and swung him around like a champion welly wanger. The poor puzzled creature flew through the air and bashed Ajay straight in the face — bottom first!

As the recipient of an unexpected rhino butt to the face, Ajay dropped the books which of course bounced straight up in the air, because that's what happens on a bouncy castle. The Glub made a dive for the books but missed and the vicious little spud soon found *it*self bouncing around out of control also!

Picture the scene dear reader — Poor Ajay nursing a bumped nose, a small rhino and an angry Glub, all bouncing around together on a bouncy castle with a Ferris wheel wedged in it. And all of them trying to grab at some bouncing books. Every time one of them landed, it sent the others flying! Jake, who was just about at the edge of his patience, watched the whole scene unfold with a sense of faint amusement. He knew exactly what had to be done. His head nodded up and down as he tried to keep track of all the bouncing, and then, at *just* the right moment, he reached out and snatched the rhino from the air as it bounced past his face. Without wasting a second, he stabbed the very surprised rhino's horn straight into the bouncy castle which immediately started to deflate with a sound like a ginormous bum-guff!

Pppppppaaaaaaaaarrrrrrrrrrppppp!!!!

The nefarious Glub looked around, its piggy little eyes frenziedly searching for the cause of the sound. The little beast was completely confused by such an impressively giant fart that wasn't coming out of *his* bottom! As far as the Glub knew, *he* was the biggest, loudest farter in all the world. So, when faced with the possibility of an even bigger farter, he became instantly infuriated and determined to find out who the imposter might be!

'Which dirty chump did that massive trump?' screeched the Glub, looking around in a fuming rage.

The distraction gave Ajay all the time he needed. He threw open the Glub's book and held it high above his head. The air shimmered again and the Glub began to swirl and whirl and whizz away back into his book. But he wasn't going home peacefully like Keith had done. He kicked and screamed and scrabbled at the air as though he could fight his way free of the magic. But once a spell has begun, nothing can stop it, and the Glub's time was up. With one last incensed wail of indignation, the nefarious Glub vanished back into the pages of his book and the flatulent little poo-tato was finally back where he belonged.

Ajay climbed down from the rapidly deflating bouncy castle, which had become more of a not-bouncy heap of yellow rubber. He opened the rhino's book and looked down at the creature which was still wriggling away under Jake's arm. 'Let's get this done,' he said, and once again the air began to shimmer like a summer's day. The rhino looked up at Jake with big sad eyes and slowly began to spiral away back into the safety of its book.

'Next time you get out,' said Jake in his sternest, most Miss Pillsbury-like voice, 'don't get mixed up with a Glub, okay! Find a nice bog troll to hang around with instead!' The rhino gave a forlorn little nod of its head and slowly faded away back into words.

The warm summer night suddenly turned cold, and the excitement that had kept the boys going was washed away by a wave of tiredness. The magical creatures had all gone. The pile of stinky clothes was no longer a mighty barricade, it was just a big mess on the floor, and the raging runaway Ferris wheel was just a broken old ride buried under a ruined bouncy castle.

'I think I'd like to go home now,' whispered Jake.

'Yeah,' smiled Ajay. 'We can watch 'Mecha-Dawn' tomorrow if you like?'

Epilogue

(That's the fancy name for the bit at the end of the book after all the action has finished!)

THE DUBSTER CRAWLED and popped and banged its way up the hill in a cloud of blue smoke. It was the last week of the summer holidays and Mum was going into town to buy herself some new shoes after two of her pairs had vanished the same night that a mysterious problem with Bisby's old plumbing had caused most of the town's laundry to be sucked into the sewers! It was also time for Jake to return the books to the library, and it was a day he had been dreading.

'I'm so glad they managed to repair all the damage that runaway wheel caused,' said mum. 'It's so lucky it short-circuited at night, imagine if it had gone wrong when there were people around!'

'Hmm,' said Jake. 'Imagine.'

After their big adventure, he and Ajay had spent days trying to coax Keith back out of his book. They had tried everything they could think of — leaving it open, waving it around, shaking it upside down, asking nicely and shouting into the pages. But nothing had worked. It was as though all the magic had run out. Jake even suggested they stick the book down the toilet, to see if that coaxed him out, but Ajay pointed out that the book still had to be returned to the library and that Mrs Crisp might not be too pleased if it came back all soggy and smelling of toilets. Eventually the boys had admitted defeat and given up trying to see their friend again. But even though they had given up trying, they never gave up hoping and Jake always made extra sure to keep the books in a pile, with 'The Curse of the Bog Troll' sat firmly on top of the other two. Just in case!

After a couple of weeks had passed by, Ajay's uncle Harish made a full recovery, and his mum came to take him home. This left Jake with plenty of time to read 'The Curse of the Bog Troll', which he was surprised to find that he enjoyed very much. He even decided that sometimes his imagination was actually better than having pictures — sometimes. He didn't dare to read the other books, just in case!

'Right then, here we are!' announced mum cheerfully as the Dubster coughed its way into the library car park, 'Oh…Oh no!'

The large wooden door was firmly closed, and an important looking sign hung around the neck of one of the stone lions.

LIBRARY CLOSED UNTIL FURTHER NOTICE. PLEASE POST ALL RETURNS THROUGH THE LETTERBOX.

Jake leapt out of the Dubster, darted past the lions and knelt down on the big granite doorstep. He used two fingers to push the letterbox open and peered inside. The lights were all switched off and there was no sign of Mrs Crisp. There was no sign of anyone at all. The dusty old praxinoscope stood on the sideboard and the chandeliers swung gently back and forth. A large pile of books lay on the floor where people had posted them through, and Jake couldn't help but notice that many of them had landed with their pages wide open....

'Post them through then, and let's get to the 'Fancy Pasty' for lunch,' called Mum.

Jake looked down at the pile of open books and grinned to himself, he could still hear Keith's voice saying, *'when you have lots of something as magical as stories all together in one place — like a library — anything could happen!'*

The End.

The Last Page

Oh, you cheeky monster! You went and did it too didn't you! You did exactly what Jake did and skipped straight to the last page to see how the story ends. I must say, I like your style! You truly are most nefarious!

So, here's the deal, I'll put a quick summary of the book below so you can read it and pretend that you've read the whole thing...but keep it our secret ok!

Jake is a magic prince who falls down a well one day. Down there he meets a snail called Trevor and the pair go on an amazing journey to the tower of Zig. Once there they battle the nefarious Glub, which is a gigantic panda with six arms and two heads. They win after Jake sings a magic song about teapots and the day is saved. Then there's a parade with confetti and Jake becomes king and they all live happily ever after!

And there you go. That's exactly what happened in this book...honest!

A note from G.A. Franks

Hello dear reader!

Thank-you for reading my book, I do hope you enjoyed reading about Jake and Ajay and their night of adventure as much as I enjoyed writing it (which was a lot!) I chose to set the story in an imaginary town called Bisby by the Sea, because it's exactly the sort of place I would like to live one day. Can you imagine living somewhere where you can get a pasty filled with popping candy and where book characters can come to life? How cool would that be!

I enjoyed writing about Bisby so much, that it got me thinking about all the other strange and wonderful people that live there and what their stories might be. Even before I had finished writing about Jake and the nefarious Glub, I already had a list of ideas and I knew that I wanted to tell more stories about the unusual goings on in Bisby by the Sea. So, watch out for more Bisby books from me in the future! And if you enjoyed this one, why not leave it a review, even if it's a short one. Your opinion is important to us and it really helps me out as an author and might mean that even more children get to explore the weird and wonderful world of Bisby by the Sea.

Take Care and Have Fun
G.A. Franks

P.S. I think Jake's mum was wrong and that comics are DEFINITELY proper reading! What do you think?

Dear reader,

We hope you enjoyed reading *Jake & The Nefarious Glub*. Please take a moment to leave a review, even if it's a short one. Your opinion is important to us.

Discover more books by G.A. Franks at https://www.nextchapter.pub/authors/ga-franks

Want to know when one of our books is free or discounted? Join the newsletter at http://eepurl.com/bqqB3H

Best regards,

G.A. Franks and the Next Chapter Team

About the Author

G.A. Franks has a life-long love of stories and writing. He is especially fond of the action-packed comic books of his youth in the 1980s. Originally from Leicestershire, he now resides in the picturesque Cotswolds with his wife and young children and works in education alongside playing bass and guitar in bands.

Discover more books by G.A. Franks at
https://www.nextchapter.pub/authors/ga-franks
Want to know when one of our books is free or discounted? Join the newsletter at
http://eepurl.com/bqqB3H
Best regards,
G.A. Franks and the Next Chapter Team

Jake & The Nefarious Glub
ISBN: 978-4-86745-590-6

Published by
Next Chapter
1-60-20 Minami-Otsuka
170-0005 Toshima-Ku, Tokyo
+818035793528

8th April 2021

www.ingramcontent.com/pod-product-compliance
Lightning Source LLC
LaVergne TN
LVHW032012070526
838202LV00059B/6421